LILY AND THE UNICORN KING

KATE GORDON

RELISH
BOOKS

CONTENTS

Cover illustration by Emma Weakley.

Cover design by A to Z Book Cover Design.

First edition July 2019.

ISBN 978-0-473-45123-3 (Kindle)

ISBN 978-0-473-45122-6 (Epub)

ISBN 978-0-473-45121-9 (Paperback)

Published by Relish Books.

www.kategordonauthor.com

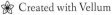 Created with Vellum

CHAPTER ONE

L ily Masterton could feel her pony gathering himself to buck before they landed over the second jump.

She gripped tighter with her knees and fisted one hand into Rainbow's long black mane. Then she took a firm hold on the reins to try and keep his head up.

But it wasn't enough.

Rainbow touched down from the jump, front feet then back feet before launching himself skyward, his back arched like a rodeo bronco.

"No, no, no!"

Lily came off the saddle, her hand in the once-wild Kaimanawa pony's mane the only thing keeping her in contact.

He landed with a dual thump of hooves then twisted up into a corkscrew movement.

That was it.

Lily flew over his shoulder, flipping to land smack on her back on the arena's sandy surface.

She lay still, eyes closed as Rainbow's hoof-beats slowed, stopped, then came back towards her. Her eyes filled with tears of frustration as the pony nuzzled her aching shoulder, all sign of his crazy antics gone.

Blinking, she swallowed hard. Why on earth did Rainbow buck every time they jumped a double?

Her chances of qualifying for the Pony Club championships were slipping away. What was his problem with a double-jump with one or no stride in between? If she couldn't fix it, they'd never be able to complete a clear round of show jumping at the qualifying trials in three weeks.

Rainbow's warm breath huffed on her face.

"All right, pony, I'm getting up now." Lily scrubbed the tears away. No one was going to see her cry. Not her two best friends, Sasha and Chloe, who both had well-schooled ponies and thankfully weren't training with her today. And especially not her mother, who would have plenty of questions about why she fell off.

"Are you okay, you silly boy?" she asked the glossy bay. It was hard to believe that only ten months earlier he'd been running wild with his herd in the mountains of New Zealand's North Island.

He shoved her gently with his nose as if to say, "Well, come on."

Lily dusted sand off her jodhpurs and swung back into the saddle. When your mum was famous in your district as a horse trainer and riding coach, one thing you learned to do was to always get back on the horse!

"Now we'll finish with something positive, right?" Lily repeated another of her mother's favourite lessons. She squeezed her legs for Rainbow to trot on. They made big half circles down the arena, the pony bending his body perfectly through the serpentine curves, his mouth gently accepting of the bit.

She'd taught him so much already, some with her mother's help and some by herself. He was no problem to saddle, shoe, or float. He worked well on the flat and really seemed to love jumping, especially when it was just the two of them, tackling the rolling hills and log jumps of the Pony Club cross-country course.

So *why* did a double fence in the show-jumping ring cause such problems? Did the saddle pinch somehow with the quickly repeated jumps?

Lily squared her shoulders and sat down to push Rainbow into his ground-eating canter. She was going to work out what the problem was and fix it.

Heading Rainbow to a single jump – a low one – her stomach was suddenly tight with anxiety. Maybe she shouldn't jump anything else in case there was something wrong with the saddle or girth. But by the time the thought was finished, Rainbow had lifted off. Instinctively, she moved with him, so they cleared the jump perfectly to land easily and canter towards the next one.

They popped over another one just as sweetly, so with a big pat on his shoulder, she asked her beloved pony to walk. She guided him out of the arena to cool off with a stroll under the gum trees which lined the driveway of her family's farm.

At the barn, she slipped off Rainbow's back. "We're going to fix this, right?"

With a gusty sigh, the pony rubbed his sweaty head on her shoulder.

"Sounds like an 'I guess so' sigh, so I'll take that."

Lily banged in through the back door, hungry and smelling of horses, and ran smack into her grandmother's arms.

"There you are, my little mokopuna." Her Māori nana

smelled of native trees and herbs and the food she loved to share with family and friends. "Come give your Kuia a hug."

Surprised but happy to find her grandmother in their kitchen, Lily wrapped her arms as far as she could around her cuddly grandmother and squeezed tight.

There was nothing as comforting as a hug with Kuia.

"Kuia! I didn't know you were coming to stay."

Her grandmother smiled at her only granddaughter. "I'm here to harvest some kawakawa while the time is right, and I might stay a while after that too. You have a beautiful patch of kawakawa plants on this farm, thanks to your clever mum and dad having the foresight to look for such things when they chose this property near the sea."

"A complete coincidence, as you very well know, Ma," came Lily's mother's voice from across the kitchen. "It was just the right farm."

"Which your ancestors told you, but you say you can't hear them," replied Kuia, repeating an argument Lily had heard all her life.

Kuia believed in the old ways, like their ancestors keeping watch over the family from the spirit world. It seemed to Lily that her mother tried not to offend Kuia while she and Dad ran the farm in a modern way.

"As much as I love my heritage, the truth is our ancestors are dead; they are no longer in the real world," said Mum, slapping a cupboard shut as if to emphasise the point.

"So you say, Tessa, so you say." Kuia snagged another hug with Lily. "Would you like to come and pick kawakawa with me before school tomorrow? There is much I can teach you."

"Oh." Lily looked over at her mother, who just smiled as if to say, 'over to you, kiddo'. "I'm not sure if I've got time,

Kuia. I am busy training Rainbow for the Pony Club championships. It's only three weeks until the qualifying competition." She needed to train before and after school if she was going to fix this jumping problem.

"Hmmm, is that right?" Kuia looked at Lily's mum and rolled her eyes in that way she had. "I seem to recall similar excuses from my own daughter many years ago, and now my granddaughter is telling me the same thing."

Kuia headed to the lounge where Lily's little brother, Liam, was playing with his toy trucks on the carpet. "Maybe this young man will accompany his Kuia."

"Brrrmmm, brrrmmm," was the two-year-old's response, making everybody laugh.

"Ah, well, it's good you know what your priorities are." Kuia eased herself down onto the rug beside Liam and began pushing a truck towards his. "But one of you is going to learn what I have to teach you before I pass from this world. Someone must take on our rongoā knowledge so you can pass it on to the next generation when the time comes."

"We've heard it all before, Mama," said Mum. "And you know I've already learnt plenty about Māori herbs and native plants."

Harrumph was Kuia's reply as Mum turned to Lily. "How did you get on today, pet?"

"Um, okay, I guess." Lily headed for the pantry.

"Fall off, did you?"

"Might have." Lily crammed a biscuit in her mouth. "Why?"

"Because there's sand all over your back."

"Oh." Lily stepped onto the back-door mat and tried to brush the sand off, embarrassed her mother had seen evidence of the fall. Another one. "Yeah, Rainbow and I have been having a few problems with the doubles."

"Anything I can help with?"

"Maybe, but I'd like to try and figure it out myself first."

"Fair enough." Tessa smiled as she sliced carrots. "You know where I am if you need me."

"Yep, I sure do." Lily gave her mum's back a quick hug. She liked that her mum never pushed her to accept help with Rainbow, unless it was for her own safety. Not like Chloe's mum who made her do extra maths lessons when Chloe was already the brightest girl in their class. It was sad Chloe never had as much time for riding as she and Sasha did.

"How long 'til dinner?"

"About twenty minutes. How about you set the table?"

"If I'm quick, can I use the computer before dinner too?"

"You better get moving," replied her mother as she swung the oven open.

Roast lamb wove its delicious smell around Lily as she typed in *show jumping troubleshooting* and scrolled through the search results. There were lots of videos of trainers fixing tricky problems, but nothing matched Rainbow's issue with double jumps.

One trainer took a Kaimanawa pony through the very basics with a series of small jumps. She groaned. No time for that, surely.

A kiss on the top of her head from her dad interrupted her.

"Hello, Lily," he said.

"Hi Dad," she replied vaguely, wondering if she'd over-faced Rainbow with jumps that were too big too soon.

Liam thumped his fist on her leg. "Illy. Illy." He grabbed her hand and tugged.

Tessa whisked dishes to the table. "Good boy, Liam, you get Lily off the computer." Lily clicked the internet browser closed. "Goodness, Lily, you're as bad as your father when you're watching something. Wash your hands now. Aren't you lucky Kuia set the table for you?"

"Oh, sorry, Mum." Lily rushed to wash and dry her hands, then kissed her grandmother's cheek as she sat down beside her. "Thanks, Kuia."

Pieces of conversation about her parents' day on the farm drifted by Lily during dinner. Dad was worried about something, but she was working out the details of how to redo the basics with Rainbow and get back to where they were now. She had three weeks. Would it be enough?

She tuned in when she heard Kuia saying something to her mother about native plants like the pōhue vine and toetoe grass. Kuia said they might strengthen Tessa's newest horse, a young bay filly who'd been tied to a fence on the road by a farm on the other side of the forest from theirs. Thin and scarred with many injuries, the filly was in a sad way when their vet had driven along the road last week. The vet immediately called the police and then Tessa, who often took on rescue horses. The police were investigating the owner who seemed to have disappeared.

Now called Kahurangi, meaning 'precious child', the filly was improving every day. Kuia thought some native plant essences might help.

"Both are good for healing physically and emotionally, for giving her the strength to stand tall and overcome the despair of her previous life. Her injuries sound more than skin-deep," Kuia said, her wrinkled eyes fixed on Tessa.

"They certainly are, the poor thing. I'll think about it, Ma." Tessa got up from the table to bring a cake for dessert.

"Didn't we use that general herbal tonic Kuia made for us when that cow went down after calving and the vet was sure wouldn't get up?" said Dad.

"Oh, did you?" Kuia replied with a smile. "And how did that go?"

"The cow was up in twenty-four hours, Ma, but it could just have easily been the antibiotics finally kicking in."

"If you say so, love." Kuia kept smiling. "But I don't think so."

Kuia's success with native plants got Lily thinking. What if there was something physically wrong with Rainbow that meant he somehow hurt deep inside with the jump-land-jump process needed to clear a double. Or what if it was an emotional hurt from being mustered out of the wild? Kuia might know something that could help him. Lily picked up the cake her mother had put in front of her and chewed as she thought.

"A thank you would be nice, Lily."

"What?"

Her mother was hot on good manners and looked at her sternly.

"Oh, sorry, Mum. Thank you. It's a yummy cake."

"Okay then. When you're done, you can clear the table and fill the dishwasher, please, while Dad and I get this little monster to bed." She grabbed Liam's hands before he fed another piece of cake to their dog, Sky, who hung out under the table every mealtime.

"I'll get the bath on," said Dad.

With Liam wriggling under one arm, Lily's mother headed out of the dining room, leaving Lily with Kuia.

Lily swallowed. "Kuia? Do you think a plant like pōhue vine can help a horse you think is well and healthy? Would it harm them if there was nothing physically wrong that needed to be fixed, but maybe there was something wrong emotionally?"

"Pōhue is helpful in many ways, but it is always better to be able to assess the creature first before deciding a possible remedy. Is this for your Rainbow?" Kuia helped her pile up the dishes.

"Yeah." Lily rinsed plates and stacked them in the dishwasher with Sky at her feet happily accepting the leftover potato from Liam's plate.

"Why do you think Rainbow has something wrong with him?"

She explained the bucking and why that might be happening.

"You are a clever mokopuna, my sweet. Yes, he may have an old trauma or perhaps an emotional scar. You and your mother train these horses with love and kindness, but they were taken from the wild, mustered by helicopter, forced into yards and trucks for the first time in their lives. That must be traumatic for them all. Maybe you can help me make a tonic tomorrow."

"Sure, that would be great, Kuia, thank you!" Lily hugged her grandmother. It was time away from training, but it could also be just what Rainbow needed.

Kuia advised Lily how to give the herbal mix to her pony. "It will be interesting to see if you find a difference with him in a few weeks."

As she finished her chores, Lily felt happier having a plan. *I'm going to go back to our jumping basics for a week*

9

and give Rainbow this tonic. Then I'll see how he is. I don't want to ask Mum for help. He's my pony, and I want to train him myself.

Kuia settled herself in front of the TV, and Lily kissed her cheek. "I'm just taking Sky down to say goodnight to the horses. I won't be long."

"Alright, love. The moon will be rising soon, and it's nearly full. Remember that marama hua brings out all the taniwha. You know they're water creatures, so don't go near the creek!"

Her grandmother's chuckle followed her out the back door.

———

Lily shivered as she latched the garden gate.

The golden light of the early summer dusk was fading into smudgy blues and purples, and one big star shone near the horizon. Jupiter, she decided, remembering some of what her father said about the night sky – he loved all that stuff. The air was filled with the never-ending roll of surf on the beach down below the big horse paddock.

If only Kuia hadn't mentioned the taniwha. She wasn't easily spooked, but gee, no one needs to hear about giant mythical lizard-like creatures and how they like to moon-bathe near water... especially when the moon was going to rise soon.

She hoped the horses weren't near the creek. Just in case.

Walking quickly, she crossed the yard. A creature flashed behind the barn. What was that?

Sky shot into view around the corner of the barn.

Oh... Her breath hissed out in relief.

"Don't scare me like that!" The black and white dog danced at her heels, his eyes sparkling. "Yeah, you can laugh. You knew it was you. I didn't."

Looking across the big paddock, she saw Rainbow and her mother's Kaimanawa mare, Gracie, over at the far fence, companionably hanging their heads over the top rail with young Kahurangi. Good, they weren't close to the rocky creek that ran through the paddock down to the private beach which curved around one corner of their farm.

The breeze brought the smell of the sea, and Lily inhaled deeply. She loved it here. Beach, forest and farm to ride on. Friends to ride with and a dog to keep her company.

"Come on, then." Sky slipped through the paddock gate at her heels. "Stay with me in case of the taniwha. They might like eating dogs too." But Sky shot away in pursuit of rabbits.

Lily broke into a jog, keen to reach the solid companionship of the horses, but then stopped as the dusky light turned silver. To the east, she watched the moon inch over the horizon. She could make out the shadows and craters. "Wow."

Dad had said it was going to be a super moon in a couple of nights. An eerie shiver trickled down her neck. If ever there was a time for taniwha, this would be it!

Rainbow nickered and walked towards Lily. "Hello, lovely boy. Are you keeping Kahurangi company?" He rubbed his forehead on her shoulder as she scratched around his ears. He sighed in contentment.

Lily ran her hands firmly over the pony, sleek and shiny in his summer coat. Down his neck, around his chest, under his belly. Was he sore? Up over his back and Rainbow just stood, calm, not a flicker of pain or discomfort.

"I don't know, mate. All I can think of doing is trying

Kuia's herbs and going back to jumping kindergarten for a few days."

Suddenly Rainbow's head went up. Snorting, he sidled under her hands.

"Easy, pony. Probably just that mad dog," Lily murmured as her hands moved over his rump, but he wouldn't settle.

She looked around. Nothing but her, the horses, the bush and their paddock. She couldn't hear anything other than the surf and her pony's breathing. But there was a sense of... something.

What... what if it's... taniwha?

CHAPTER TWO

Suddenly a deep rumbling noise interrupted the everyday sound of the Tasman Sea meeting the shore.
What the heck...?

Another rolling rumble. It seemed to come from down near the beach.

She froze. What was happening?

The horses' ears were pricked towards the sound as it got louder. Lily stood at Rainbow's shoulder, drawing strength from his presence. He wasn't trembling or running from the noise, so it wasn't too scary...for him.

The ground trembled under her feet, echoing the deepening roar.

Her heart jumped.

Was it an earthquake? Should she run to the house? Tell her parents?

A shrill neigh cut through the night.

She looked around quickly. Which horse was that? Gracie and Rainbow were right here. Kahurangi was just over the fence, also facing the beach.

More whinnies, some small and frightened, among the strange, continuous rumbling from the beach.

Are those foals? Are they hurt?

Lily spoke out loud as if the horses could answer. "How can there be foals? We haven't got any, so whose horses are they?"

More shrill whinnies had Lily gulping down her fear of the unknown. She grabbed a handful of mane and vaulted onto Rainbow's bare back. "We have to go see."

He moved forward willingly as she squeezed her legs. "I don't know what it is, Rainbow, but if a horse is hurt or something, we have to help if we can."

Lily nudged Rainbow into a canter across the silvery, moonlit grass. Thankful they'd done lots of bareback work without bridle or even a halter, she asked him to halt at the gate by leaning her weight back slightly. A nudge here, pressure there, and they quickly navigated the gate onto the track through native trees down to the beach.

"Just walk, pony." She urged him forward. "It's a bit dark through here. Your eyesight is probably better than mine, but no point stumbling over tree roots if we don't need to."

She could hear the rumbling over the crunching of Rainbow's hooves as he walked briskly down the gravel track. Anxious whinnies still rang out.

Confused by whose horses could possibly be on their private beach, Lily also couldn't fathom what was making that incredible roar.

They stepped out of the trees onto the sand, bright with moonlight.

"Oh. My. Goodness." Lily's mouth dropped open.

Horses.

Everywhere.

Foals and mares. Bigger horses – geldings or stallions maybe. Pale greys, dappled greys, marbled silver-greys and little foals with darker, almost black coats. All milling around in restless groups while the roaring sound seemed to come from behind them right down by the surf.

Hold on.

Those weren't horses...

Where she expected to see the familiar lines of their heads, there was something... Something long and pointed...and only seen in books and fairy tales.

Dumbfounded, she asked her pony, "Are they *unicorns?*"

With a friendly nicker, Rainbow started towards the closest group.

He touched noses with a light dappled-grey unicorn who had a foal tucked in close to her flank.

Trembling, Lily had eyes only for the ivory spike rising from the unicorn's forehead. The twisted curves caught the silvered light. The tip was so sharp, so lethal. Would she use it on Rainbow to protect her foal? Would the others?

Now they were surrounded by unicorns armed with those deadly spikes. Lily sat frozen on Rainbow's back. How would they escape if the unicorns decided to attack?

The mare whuffled a greeting just like Rainbow would and Lily relaxed a fraction.

They seemed friendly. So far.

But where had they come from?

She nudged Rainbow forward across the sand, the constantly moving groups of unicorns around them. Closer to the sea, there was...

She gasped and pointed even though there was no one else to see.

It was...a kind of chasm, a gaping hole in the beach just metres from the surf. The roaring sound came directly from the hole from which a very dark unicorn staggered then collapsed.

Two larger unicorns galloped towards their fallen colleague, throwing up sand as they skidded to a halt. The silvery one nuzzled the dark unicorn, obviously encouraging it to get up. The other darkly dappled one tossed his head, and the unicorns milling around Lily galloped to that inexplicable hole in the beach, turned and formed a row as if on command. They kicked sand into the hole with their rear hooves, but from what Lily could see in the ever-brightening moonlight, it didn't make any difference to the size of the hole although maybe the pulsing sound was a bit quieter.

Without the unicorns gathered around, Lily felt suddenly exposed. A girl and her pony watching mythical creatures in some desperate struggle on her family's private beach.

Then the head-tossing, dark-dappled unicorn saw them and charged!

"Run, Rainbow, run!" Lily kicked her pony's sides and tugged on his mane. But he stood there calmly, watching the large unicorn gallop towards them with his head lowered and that spike ready to run them through.

"Rainbow, come on!" Frantic, she kicked and punched Rainbow's neck, rump, anywhere she could reach, but nothing.

Should she get off and run? She looked around. The native bush which ran down to the beach was quite a way off. Fast runner though she was, she was no match for an angry unicorn on the soft sand.

Swinging back to face the terrifying unicorn, she couldn't believe Rainbow was just standing there, waiting for certain hurt. Tucking herself tightly against her pony's neck, she closed her eyes. Those thundering hooves came closer.

Then...

Furious snorting and a deep voice. "Who are you?"

Eyes popping open in disbelief, Lily sat up.

Did the unicorn just talk to me?

The huge dark grey unicorn swung its spike frighteningly close to Rainbow's beautiful head. "Answer me!" It was angry. "Who are you and why are you here?"

"Um," she squeaked. "I'm Lily and this is our beach."

The silvery unicorn thundered up, spraying sand over them all. Rainbow stayed steady beneath her, simply snorting the sand off his face.

"It's a human, as you can see, Sire! Spying for Abellona, perhaps." The first unicorn spat the words out angrily.

"I see a girl on a pony, Sigvard," the silvery one replied. "There is no cause for alarm at this point."

Hearing his deep yet strangely soothing voice, Lily's terror of being run through by a unicorn horn lessened. He towered over her and Rainbow, but somehow he didn't frighten her. On the contrary, she found herself reaching out a hand to him.

He lowered his head so she could touch his muzzle.

"Oh!" Lily snatched her hand away.

"It's alright, child. I feel it too."

"Like a tingling?"

He nodded.

Beside him, Sigvard stamped his hooves. "Not again, Ambrosius. This constant desire to interact with humans is dangerous."

"Hush, Sigvard, we do not know if the child can help."

Lily only had eyes for the unicorn called Ambrosius. She placed her hand flat on his cheek, her gaze locked with his and away from that polished spike which shone in the moonlight.

There it was again. A warm tingle. Flowing from her hand, up her arm. "Wow. It's...it's..."

"Indescribable?" The chuckle in the unicorn's voice made it sound like he was smiling.

Lily's hand moved over the silky coat of his cheek and neck. It felt just like Rainbow's, but with that amazing feeling, kind of a magical warmth. "You're right, I can't describe it, but it's wonderful."

"We simply call it a connection. It is wonderful and very rare, despite what Sigvard says. You are only the third person in my lifetime with whom I have felt it."

"Wow," Lily whispered. She didn't know what to say. *What do you say to a unicorn when he tells you something like that?*

"Sire!" Sigvard spoke with urgency. "This is all very well, but we need to get off this beach. And what about Brökk?"

Lily had almost forgotten he and the other unicorns were milling around as she petted the one who seemed to be the herd's leader. Her whole body quivered gently as the warm connection wove through her. It was like when she realised that she loved her pony Rainbow more than anything else in the world. Yet somehow more.

Ambrosius sighed as he lifted his head away from Lily's hand. He rested his muzzle ever so gently on her head for a moment before turning to his colleague. "Yes, Sigvard. As you know, you cannot seek a *connection*. They simply exist. Can we not take this as a positive sign? But I agree, we do need to move. Have the herd continue trying to conceal the portal as best they can. I will see if Lily can help us with where we can take Brökk to rest."

With a snort of acknowledgement, Sigvard thundered back towards the giant hole on the beach where Lily could see the other nearly black unicorn still lay.

The silvered one cleared his throat to draw her attention. "I will speak quickly. Let me introduce myself more formally. I am Ambrosius, King of the herd of Västerbotten, from the lands you know as Scandinavia. We are being pursued by a determined and devious sorceress named Abellona and seek to get as far away as possible from our homeland. We have a little time, we don't know how long, a few days perhaps, before we expect her to follow us through the portal made by our mage Brökk." Ambrosius nodded his spike towards the fallen unicorn. "The question is, can you help us find somewhere secluded to rest and allow Brökk to heal? Obviously, we do not know your land as we know our own."

Lily opened her mouth but had no words. He – a unicorn king – wanted her – a twelve-year-old girl – to help his *herd* of unicorns hide from an angry *witch*?

"Me?" she squeaked. "You want me to help?"

"Yes, Lily, if you can," he replied calmly.

"But...but I've got to qualify Rainbow for the Pony Club championships..."

"Surely," Ambrosius said with a smile in his voice, "that is not at this very moment."

Rainbow shuffled his feet in the sand, and Lily smiled ruefully. "Um, no."

"That is good to hear." The unicorn king moved to face his herd. Most were kicking sand into the hole, lessening the intense roaring sound. A few were beside Brökk, the moonlit phosphorescence of the waves gently curling onto the sand creating a backdrop for the stricken unicorn. Foals stood quietly with their mothers, heads hanging.

"The foals are tired," Lily said, her mind reeling with all she was seeing and hearing. The herd needed help to keep the foals safe, but how?

"They are. We need to get out of this bay to somewhere that other humans won't find us. Can you think of somewhere we might move to? To save us heading off into the unknown and potentially meet more people who may not be as accepting as you are."

Oh heck. Lily thought hard.

"Oh!"

"Yes?" said Ambrosius eagerly.

"The farm where Kahurangi was found. There's no people, no stock." She pointed away to the far end of the bay. "It's through the trees in that direction, and you don't pass any other farms or houses on the way."

"That sounds promising. Let me talk with Sigvard. I want us all to be somewhere much safer by dawn." He trotted over to the others.

A sharp whistle blasted through the night.

"Oh, geez, Rainbow. That's Dad's sheep-dog whistle." Lily looked up at the night sky. The moon was up a good way from the horizon. How long had she and Rainbow been out here?

She nudged her pony to follow the unicorn. "We'll quickly make sure they know where they're going, okay?" Rainbow snorted in reply as he broke into a trot. She squeezed her legs to grip on. "Then we better get home."

"Good, you're here." Ambrosius turned to Lily as she stopped beside him. "Can you please explain as best you can where this deserted farm is? Sigvard will send Guilio up to scout ahead for us."

"Who's gwe-le-o?"

A white, winged creature stepped from among the unicorns working on the portal. "I am Guilio, the guardian pegasus of this fine herd."

Lily gasped. A winged horse! How had she not seen him among the unicorns?

The pegasus stopped in front of Rainbow and dropped his head as if bowing to Lily. "What landmarks should I seek?"

Lily closed her eyes, trying to visualise how to find the farm from the air, which wasn't something she'd ever had to do before. She'd hate to get this wrong.

"Okay, I've got this," she whispered to herself.

She opened her eyes and pointed. "When you leave the beach at that end, after a little while the bush – the native trees – become pine forest. Through the pines you'll come to the dead-end part of a dead-end road. Follow that road until the first driveway on the..." She paused to think. "Left. The driveway winds up a long hill. I've never been up there, so don't know much about the farm other than it's among hills and has lots of tree-filled gullies, which seems like a good hiding place."

Another whistle sounded. It was closer, but still up in the horse paddock as far as Lily could tell.

"I have to go!" She turned to Ambrosius. "Can I come and see you tomorrow? Early, before school. Just to make sure you're okay."

"Of course," he replied. "Now you go. And thank you!"

"Good luck!" She waved and nudged Rainbow to canter along the beach. She couldn't risk Dad coming down to the beach to look for her and then seeing the unicorns. And finding their chasm thing.

Ambrosius said humans must not know about them and some people would just want to catch the unicorns to keep them on display. Not that Dad would probably be like that, but I won't risk it.

At least the noise was getting less the more sand they kicked into it, but a big hole like that was pretty obvious on a normally smooth beach. Mum and Liam liked to walk along the beach most days. She had no idea how the unicorns would fill it or hide it but hoped they would sort it out. And soon.

She glanced back. The silvery creatures were moving along the beach to the far end, several walking close beside a slow-moving darker one. Brökk. At least he could stand up now.

Will some rest be enough to heal him? What will happen if the witch somehow followed them?

She shivered, icy fear tingling down her spine.

"I don't even want to think about that, Rainbow." They reached the track through the trees, and she pressed him into a fast canter. "We're going to be busy enough with your training, herbs with Kuia, and trying to fit in seeing the unicorns tomorrow as it is. Lucky it's the holidays the day after tomorrow."

They reached the gate.

"There you are!" Dad's voice boomed from behind the dazzling light of his big torch.

"Don't blind us, Dad." Lily slipped off Rainbow to go through the gate.

He flicked the torchlight away from them. "What have you been doing? Why were you on the beach? And after dark too." He sounded worried.

Rainbow followed Lily as she walked up to her father and grabbed his hand. "The moon was amazing, Dad."

And so were the unicorns, but I can't tell you about them. Oh heck, how am I going to keep them a secret from Sasha and Chloe?

"I just wanted to see it from the beach. You know how the waves light up with phosphorescence?"

As she hoped, that got her father talking about the science of the little sea creatures in the waves being fluorescent.

They walked back across the paddock, her hand tucked in her dad's big, work-roughened one. All Lily could think about was how were the unicorns getting on finding the abandoned farm.

Even if they just hide in the bush away from the beach, that might be okay for a while. I wonder if Ambrosius – what an amazing name – would mind if I told Sasha and Chloe. I'd feel mean if I didn't. They'd tell me if one of them met a herd of unicorns, I'm sure of it. I don't think I can keep something like this a secret from them. It's just too exciting.

She patted Rainbow goodnight at the gate back into the stable yard, as Dad latched the gate.

Yawning, she followed Dad into the house. She'd figure out whether or not to tell her friends tomorrow. She was sure they would be able to keep the secret safe.

CHAPTER THREE

*B*rrrrp-a-do! Brrrrp-a-do!
      Lily woke with a start, eyes open in the dark. The alarm of her mobile phone chirped again. She fumbled to stop it playing a third time and hoped the volume was quiet enough that no one else in the house were woken.

Her tummy was tight with excitement and a strange fear that meeting the unicorns and pegasus last night was all, somehow, in her imagination. Lily rushed to dress super quietly then eased her door open to listen.

Silence, except... A low droning sound from the bedroom next door had her wondering for a precious minute.

Oh, it's Kuia snoring.

Lily padded to the back door, grabbed a torch, and slipped on her boots and a jacket. With a quick plea that Sky, with his supersonic doggie hearing, was still sound asleep by her parents' bed, she was out into the pitch dark and away down to the barn as fast and as quietly as she could.

Before she'd turned out her light last night, Lily had decided she couldn't not tell her best friends. She'd sent them a text, asking them to meet her at her barn with their ponies at five o'clock the next morning.

That was now. But what if Sasha and Chloe didn't come? What if they couldn't get out of their houses without being heard? And even if they did come, she didn't know how to tell her friends about the unicorns. Would they even believe her until they'd seen the unicorns themselves? She could still hardly believe it herself that real-life unicorns had asked her for help.

"What the heck, Lily!" Sasha Graham's voice hissed from the dark as Lily rushed into the barn.

"Shoot! Don't scare me like that." Lily eased the door closed and turned on the torch. "Why are you in here?

"Duh, it's cold outside." Sasha's face glowed eerily in the torchlight, her eyes intent on Lily. "Are you for real? Asking us to come and meet you before dawn?"

Lily jumped as the door creaked open. Her other best friend Chloe Cho appeared. "What on earth's going on? I've got to be back home for breakfast and a piano lesson in two hours."

"Well?" Sasha demanded.

Lily took a breath. "Last night..." *How best to tell them?* "I came across something very special, and I want to show you."

"In the middle of the night?" Sasha's voice went up in disbelief.

"It's very early morning, so don't be picky, Sash. But it's really important and really secret."

"It better be important, Lil," said Chloe in her gentle voice. "Because my mum's already threatened to sell Angel if she thinks I'm not studying hard enough. I can't afford to get into any trouble."

Lily's heart sank. How could Chloe's mother say Angel might be sold? The palomino mare was the loveliest pony and just perfect for Chloe.

What if she was getting her friends into trouble by involving them with the unicorns? She didn't know what was going to happen. What if the witch followed the herd to New Zealand?

But Sasha and Chloe were her best friends. *How can I keep the unicorns a secret? They're just so beautiful, so magical. Every pony-mad girl's dream, right?*

She took a breath. "It's not trouble, I promise." She crossed her fingers and silently willed it to be true. "Come with me for a quick ride into the pine forest. I've got to be back to pick herbs with Kuia, so we'll be as quick as we can, but you really need to see for yourself."

Lily grabbed Rainbow's tack, and Sasha eased the barn door open. She always wanted to be first. "Come on then. Turn off that torch. The sooner our eyes adjust to the dark, the better."

The girls' ponies were tethered by the barn, and both Rainbow and Gracie were leaning over the gate to see what was going on. Lily slipped the reins of Rainbow's bridle over his neck and asked him to move away from the gate. Gracie followed, letting the others come through into the horse paddock. Chloe held Angel and Sasha's pony Tommy while Sasha helped Lily fumble around in the dark to tack up Rainbow.

"Sorry I haven't groomed you, Rainbow," Lily whispered as she pulled the girth tight. "I'll do it really well after school." She swung up in the saddle and looked around. Gee, it was dark. The moon was nearly down, and there was no sign of dawn on the horizon. She hoped it might have been getting a little bit lighter by now. But she had the torch.

"Where are we going?" Sasha hissed once she mounted her chestnut gelding. "You know, we really can't be late back for Chloe."

"Like I said, through the pine forest." Lily led the way across the big horse paddock, Gracie tagging along behind. "I'm sure we can get where I want to go and back in time."

"Oh, Lil, it's going to be so dark in there," Chloe said quietly over the padding of the ponies' hooves across the short grass. "Will the ponies be okay?

"They can see better than we can," Sasha replied.

"We can use the torch once we're among the trees." Lily patted her jacket pocket. Yep, the torch was still there.

Lily looked intently at the forbidding mass of trees beyond the far fence-line of the big horse paddock. Oh fudge, it was really dark!

"So it's not a new horse, then." Sasha's voice sounded less antsy now she was riding her beloved Tommy. "Not that that would be much of a secret or involve riding through the forest in the pitch dark when we normally have to ask permission to ride there in regular daylight." She didn't sound cross, more excited. Sasha loved adventures.

Lily's heart sank as she looked at Sasha, just able to make out her friend's smiling face under her riding helmet. "Oh, you're right, Sash. I was so set on introducing you to...this special thing, that I forgot about that."

Chloe nudged Angel closer to Rainbow. "We're meeting someone? Who?"

"Someone really special." She reached out to grab her

friend's hand and squeezed. "It will be worth it, and you'll get home in time, promise. We can leave Angel with our guys if you haven't got time to take her back to the Pony Club paddocks."

They reached the gate into the forest, and Lily dismounted to deal with its fiddly latch.

"Are you sure about this, Lil?" Chloe looked down at Lily as her golden pony stepped lightly through the gate.

A tremor of excitement and nerves made Lily's hands shake as she shut the gate. Sasha was right, they weren't meant to ride in the forest without permission, but she couldn't wait to see the unicorns again. *I hope I'm doing the right thing. Surely Ambrosius won't mind me bringing my friends.* They simply had to know about the unicorns as well. It was too special not to share. Decision confirmed.

She mounted Rainbow and fished the torch out of her pocket. "Yes, I'm sure." The torchlight showed a gravel road through the tall pine trees snaking away and up a long slope.

"Come on then." They walked the ponies three abreast, Lily in the middle. "The track's pretty good. Let's trot."

Lily felt alert to every possible sight and sound as the scent of pine trees wove round them. Her vision was narrowed to the bright beam of the torch showing the stony, car-width track, and the dark green pines on either side. The ponies trotted eagerly alongside each other, the odd snort and jingle of a bit the only other sound over the trotting hooves.

"Possum!" Sasha pointed up into the trees where the torchlight reflected off a pair of blinking eyes.

"Yuck," said Chloe with feeling.

They reached the top of a long slope and a T-junction. "Left," said Lily without hesitation.

"Are we going onto Sanderson Road?" Sasha asked.

"That's right."

Then it was back to just the sound of trotting hooves and the intense contrast between the torchlight and the darkness around them.

Lily was thankful her friends weren't asking more questions. She wanted to check her watch for the time, but obviously couldn't shine the torch away from the track. Hopefully they were doing okay. It wasn't far to the dead-end of Sanderson Road now. *But how long will it take us to find the unicorns on the farm?*

They trotted steadily down the other side of the long slope of pines. Lily thought they weren't far from the gate onto the road.

Sasha must have been thinking the same thing. "What if the gate's padlocked?"

"We'll just have to jump it, won't we?" Lily wasn't stopping now. "You know we've jumped the fence beside the gate before."

"In daylight."

"Think of it as a new challenge." Lily tried to put a smile in her voice but wondered if maybe she was leading them on a crazy adventure.

Reaching the gate, Sasha nudged Tommy up to it as Lily shone the torch. "It's not padlocked!"

"Whew!"

Ponies all safely through, they trotted briskly up the middle of the empty gravel road. The torch beam reached across the wide grass verge to show continuous wire and batten fences, and then a gateway on the left.

Relieved they'd got this far without any delays, Lily said, "We're turning in here."

"Here?" Sasha asked as she followed Lily up the weed-lined, dirt driveway. "Isn't this where Kahurangi was found? With that bad guy?"

"Yes, but he's gone now. The farm is empty. The someone I want you to meet is on the farm somewhere. Hopefully they'll be pretty obvious, and we can find them quickly."

"You don't actually know where they are?" Chloe sounded anxious as she bought Angel up beside Rainbow.

"Not exactly, but I'm sure they won't be too hard to find." She crossed her fingers around Rainbow's reins.

The three ponies crested the first rise of the long drive and slowed to a walk. Lily shone the torch from side to side.

To the right, a falling-down farmhouse and rusty dog kennels. Lily shivered. She was glad the mean man was gone, but the feeling of sadness and pain lingered. It didn't feel like a nice place to have suggested to the unicorns, but at least no one would find them here for now.

In front of them, the rough driveway continued into the blackness. Swinging left, the torch beam found an open gate in a sagging fence-line. Her eyes followed the light across the paddock, and then silvery horse-like shapes appeared.

"They *are* here," Lily whispered, relieved to have found the unicorns so quickly. *But should they have hidden themselves better from anyone coming onto the farm?*

Outside the beam of the torch, faint circles of light glowed around each unicorn. How and why did they do that?

"Wow," Sasha stage-whispered. "Did you bring us to see these horses... Oh, they're not horses..."

"No, they're not horses, Sash. They're *unicorns!*" Lily whispered back, still feeling weird that she was even saying such a thing. Unicorns were for legends and fairy tales, not real life. She felt Chloe's hand reach for hers and clasped it.

"It's okay, Chlo. I met them, well, one, the main one, last night."

Sasha stood up in her stirrups to look around more. "Holy moly, Lil, how did you not burst wanting to tell us?"

"Of course I wanted to, but it seemed easier to just show you. Would you have believed me?"

"Not a chance," Sasha replied. "Turn the torch off. There's enough moonlight."

With the harsh beam of the torch gone, the golden nimbus of light around each unicorn created magical circles dotted around the field.

"Amazing." Sasha's voice was hushed with wonder.

Lily glanced at Chloe and smiled. The moonlight showed her gentle, quiet friend was clearly entranced by the sight before them.

As the night before, the big warrior unicorn charged. This time Lily felt fairly sure he'd stop in time, but she moved Rainbow to stand in front of Chloe and Angel in case Sigvard frightened them.

"It's you again, is it?" said the unicorn. "I wonder the wisdom of allowing Ambrosius to get close to another human, but our leader seems set on fostering the connection he says he has with you. And now you bring others with you." Sigvard snorted with disgust.

"I said I would come, and you know I only want to help." Lily realised as she spoke that she truly did want help. She had a lot of other things going on, but somehow, overnight, the unicorns had become very important to her. Especially Ambrosius. "I'm sure the others want to help just as much as I do."

Out of the corner of her eye, she saw Sasha nodding,

even though Sasha didn't yet know anything about the unicorns or the evil sorceress Ambrosius mentioned last night.

"Could you take us to Ambrosius, please?"

"*He* will insist upon it." Sigvard's words left no doubt that he disagreed with his king, but then Lily noticed he kept looking at Sasha. Why? "Our sire is with Brökk," he continued. "Follow me."

In the light glowing from the king's lieutenant, they trotted across the rolling pasture. Unicorns grazed or rested alone, in pairs of mares and foals, and in small groups. Like her friends, Lily couldn't stop looking around, drinking up the sights and sounds of the herd.

"The foals are so sweet!" whispered Chloe. "Some are really tiny. How on earth did they get here? How did *any* of them get here?"

"I saw them arrive, but honestly have no idea how the process worked," replied Lily. "I'm sure Ambrosius will explain more this morning."

Chloe looked at Lily. "Okay but remember we can't stay too long."

"Yep, keeping that in mind."

Sigvard trotted beside Sasha and Tommy. Again, Lily saw him glancing at her friend. For a unicorn who wasn't keen on people, she thought he seemed very interested in Sasha.

They reached Ambrosius and Brökk, the unicorn king standing guard over the herd's magical leader resting on the ground. Lily sensed a great sadness around the pair and walked her pony to stand beside Ambrosius, wondering how she could help them.

"Ah, Lily, you found us." There was that smile in his

voice again. It bought a kind of warmth to her heart, inexplicable but true.

She reached out to run her hand along the strong crest of his neck. His silvery mane was long and tangled. *It could do with a good brush.* She smiled at the idea of grooming the huge unicorn stallion. A deep tingle ran down her arm into her chest and Lily closed her eyes, the feeling of happiness real as the connection ran through her.

It's okay. He's here. I didn't imagine him. I didn't imagine this.

"It's good to see you, Lily." Ambrosius' rich voice rumbled around and through her as Lily's eyes flicked open and locked onto his.

The sense of connection she'd felt last night was, if anything, stronger now.

She swallowed and said the words she had been worried about saying ever since she'd woken that morning. "I hope you don't mind that I brought my friends with me, Ambrosius. To meet you is the most amazing experience of my life, and to share it with my best friends, well, I couldn't think of anything better."

His eyes locked on hers. "I trust you, Lily. If you trust your friends to keep our secret, then I say we shall be glad of any assistance they can provide in this land which is so foreign to us. I must say the grazing is very good, and our mares are pleasantly surprised at how quickly they feel rested and well-fed."

Tears of relief welled, and Lily swallowed hard before she could reply. "Oh, thank goodness you're not upset with me." She wiped her eyes. "I'd better introduce my friends then. This is Sasha on her chestnut Tommy, and this is Chloe on her palomino Angel."

"Pleased to meet you, Sasha and Chloe." Ambrosius bowed his head. "In turn, let me introduce Brökk."

Bathed in the light emanating from his colleagues, the stricken unicorn raised his head and greeted them in a croaky voice.

Lily slipped from Rainbow's saddle, handing his reins to Chloe. "Brökk, I've been so worried about you. May I see your injuries?" She stepped closer to the darkest unicorn of them all. "My grandmother is a great natural healer, and she might be able to make a remedy to help you."

Brökk nodded and Ambrosius moved so his light helped Lily see better.

She ignored Sigvard's restless movements behind Ambrosius but figured what it was about. "I'm not going to tell my grandmother about you, of course, Sigvard. I simply will say something about a friend's pony being injured."

She knelt beside Brökk. His breathing was laboured as his big dark eyes assessed her. She sensed a powerful force within him, but also great pain and tiredness. "How are you injured, Brökk? I can see burns on your leg." From his knee down, Brökk's foreleg was blistered with very little normal-looking skin or hair.

"Ja." His voice was raspy. "I have many burns." A deep cough sounded painful. "Damage inside too, I think."

Lily looked up at Ambrosius. "I think it's going to take more than rest for him to heal. Unless there's some magic I don't know about."

Ambrosius nodded. "We have our empath Mikaela spending most of her time with Brökk. She can generate feelings of strength and healing which help, but she needs to rest too. Your idea of your grandmother's remedy is also good. We must do all we can to assist Brökk. If Abellona follows us when Brökk is not at full strength, we are in grave danger. When do you think you can get back to us with something to help Brökk?"

Lily saw Sasha and Chloe glancing at each other and back to Ambrosius. They looked confused. She felt like she'd made them jump into the middle of a story without reading the first chapters.

CHAPTER FOUR

mbrosius was waiting for Lily's answer. "Hopefully tonight," she said. "Kuia asked me to help this afternoon with some herbs that I want to try for Rainbow, so I'll ask her about this too. I'll just have to get out once everyone's gone to bed."

"I'll come with you, Lil," Sasha said straightaway. "You shouldn't be riding through the forest alone at night."

"I can accompany you if that helps." Sigvard looked at Sasha as he spoke. "If you explain what path you reach to get here, I will be there to light your way."

Sasha smiled at the big warrior unicorn. "Much easier than Lily trying to carry that big torch like she did this morning."

"I'd like to come too," Chloe said quietly, "but I don't know if I can get to and from the Pony Club to get Angel and have time to ride over here."

"Oh gosh, thinking of time." Lily checked her watch. "It's six o'clock. We better think about heading back soon. But you can leave Angel at our place now, Chlo. I'll tell Dad something like she's being harassed by another pony at the club grazing."

"Are you sure he won't mind?"

"We've offered to have Angel graze with us before. It's your mum who doesn't want to."

"That's enough about grazing," Sasha butted in. "I've just got to know: how do you make the light around you?"

"It's nothing," rumbled Sigvard, standing close to Tommy. "Unicorn foals can do this from birth. The first skill we all master is how to control our glow so we can hide with our mothers and not reveal the herd to our enemies."

"But," Sasha responded quickly, "if you're in a strange place, don't you want to stay secret? Why shine your light?"

Sigvard replied, "Because our guardians like Guilio, Mikaela and her kind cannot sense any enemies here."

"That is not to say," Ambrosius added, "that there is not magic here. Mikaela, who is developing the most extraordinary sensory powers we have ever seen among all the unicorn herds, tells us there is indeed some kind of old magic in this land that she is yet to understand. But she does not sense any evil, hence we feel comfortable to relax and glow at the current time."

"There's so much I'd like to know about your life, Sigvard." Sasha's voice held a passion Lily hadn't heard for months. Not since Sasha first told them about some problems at home.

"It would give me great pleasure to show you around our homeland, young one, although how we might ever venture there together is unknown to me at this point in time."

"Oh, Lily, Chloe," Sasha turned to grin at them, "wouldn't that be amazing?"

"Amazing!" replied Lily, silently agreeing with Sigvard

that it was a complete mystery how they could ever see where the unicorns lived.

"Excuse me," came Chloe's gentle voice. "If Sasha can ask questions, can I ask one too?"

Ambrosius nodded. "Of course."

She swallowed. "If you aren't from New Zealand, how did you get here?"

"Brökk can create a chasm under the earth through which we travel," he replied.

Lily saw Chloe's eyes go wide with wonder as Ambrosius continued, "It would be clearer if we explain why we're here."

Lily looked at her watch again. "Would it be possible to explain super quickly, please? We really do need to go soon."

Ambrosius nodded. "As Lily knows, we are the herd of Västerbotten and have escaped our homeland to try and avoid capture by our former protector, the witch Abellona."

Chloe gasped.

"For many long years, she has feuded with her twin brother Perseus. We unicorn herds are mere pawns in their games of war, which they move from one land to the next on a whim." Ambrosius paused, his face solemn. "For most of this time, Abellona has tried to enslave us, for we are one of just three unicorn herds who remain free. She seeks to pitch us in battle against our own kind."

Lily's chest tightened with fear hearing this new information. That witch sounded horrible.

"Our patron Celestina, the kind-hearted younger sister of the twins, is no longer able to protect us as she was captured when Abellona and Perseus recently made a rare decision to work together. Now they are back to their deadly feud, and we are Abellona's next target, hence the decision to flee as far from our homeland as we could. One day we will try and return to free Celestina, and maybe stop Abellona and Perseus, but for now we seek to hide from Abellona and regain our full strength."

"Wow," Sasha said shakily. "And I thought my home life was difficult! Do you think this Abellona will follow you here?"

Sigvard spoke. "We expect so. With the help of Celestina's guardian dog Pudersnö who fortunately managed to avoid being captured with her, Abellona was distracted from monitoring our region for a few days. But it's only a matter of time before she attempts to follow us through the chasm."

"Oh, no..." Chloe pressed her hand to her mouth. "She could get here?"

Ambrosius nodded. "We expect she will. While this farm is a fine place for us to rest for a day or two, maybe three, we will need a more secluded place to move to. And that's why we ask for your assistance."

Sigvard jumped in. "What we seek from you is the opportunity to exploit Abellona's distaste of humans. We wish to disguise the herd in some way near a large enough group of humans for a sufficient period of time for Brökk to return to full health. With the greatest of luck, perhaps Abellona will lose interest in searching for us at the present time and think of another ploy to take on her scheming twin."

Lily looked at her friends. They looked as stunned as she felt.

Disguise the herd?

"Um, how..." Lily stuttered. "How in the world could we do that?"

"Yeah," said Sasha, "it's not like we've got any magical

powers." She shook her head in bewilderment. "Sounds like you need big magic to take on this witch."

Ambrosius touched his muzzle gently on Lily's shoulder. "There's a lot for you to comprehend, we know. But we also need to make some decisions and quickly."

Lily locked gazes with the unicorn king, feeling more frightened every moment. "What's it like for the unicorns the witch has captured?"

"And the pegasuses she's enslaved." The pegasus standing guard not far away spoke up. "A fate worse than death."

"Guilio, I'm very sad to say, knows from personal experience," Ambrosius explained. "His brother Galen and Galen's mate Xanthe were captured by Abellona some years ago. Galen is forced to carry Abellona upon his back as she takes to the skies to hunt his comrades. The alternative is he must witness Abellona's torturous treatment of poor Xanthe, which becomes more unbearable for our beloved Galen than having to be a traitor to one's herd and friends."

Lily felt sick to her stomach. "That's just...awful." She sniffed back tears that threatened to fall. "Of course I'll help. If I can." She glanced at her friends, who both looked pale and worried. "We all will." They nodded. "I'm just not sure how."

Sigvard responded, his voice brisk. "We think our best defence while Brökk heals is to hide the herd near humans in the hope the overwhelming smell of people will prevent Abellona's attack dog from finding our scent and leading her to us. Our sensory, Mikaela, will provide some advance warning, but we cannot remain here, so close to the chasm."

Lily looked from one to the other. "And like last night, you think because we're locals, we might be able to help?"

Sigvard snorted with impatience. "Well, do you know

the area, or not? We don't have time to search for a suitable hiding place every night and leave the herd more vulnerable to attack. Obviously we cannot search by day."

Ambrosius added, "Normally Brökk would be able to close the chasm fully behind us, but this was a much, much longer journey than we have ever undertaken. He nearly killed himself to get us all here safely and didn't have the energy or magic left to reach this far across the world and close the chasm completely, and thus help protect our destination from others trying to detect it. As you can see, the next priority is to get the herd to as safe a place as we can. Then Brökk can have the time to heal. I'm sure he will, with enough time."

"Or we'll never get home again." Guilio's bleak voice came from the edge of the trees where he stood watch.

Tears welled again as Lily looked at Guilio and back to the two massive unicorns. *That's too sad to even think about.* The weight of their expectations settled on her. *There is so much at stake.*

Lily puzzled over the need for a suitable hiding place. *If only I could think of somewhere!*

She looked up at her friends on their ponies. "What do you think?

Chloe's dark eyes were worried as she looked at Lily. "Do you think we could do an internet search in the library at lunchtime? Then ride out tomorrow morning to check any place that looks suitable?"

Sigvard cleared his throat with a deep cough. "Well, that sounds fine, but we're in somewhat of a hurry."

That reminded Lily to check the time. *We need to go!*

He continued. "Do you have any immediate possibilities for a place we can move the herd to tonight?"

Lily sighed. "It's not that simple, because we don't know

every farm, park or area of native bush around Whale Bay. It was just lucky I remembered that this farm is empty of people and animals at the moment."

Chloe spoke. "Ambrosius, didn't you say it might be up to three days before *she* – I can't even say her name, she sounds so awful – could get here? Do you expect she could travel through the chasm faster than you did?"

"No, her army would travel at around the same speed," the unicorn king replied.

"So if you didn't move tonight, that's okay?"

"I believe so, yes. Sigvard is just trying to get us to the safest possible place as quickly as we can."

"We understand that, but we need to think about what you've told us," Sasha jumped in. "We have to go to school today, but we'll search on the internet at lunchtime. Like Chloe said, we can ride out tomorrow morning to check the most likely possibilities. You probably can't move tonight, but possibly tomorrow night, or even the night after – Sunday. Thank goodness today is the last day of school for six weeks. Christmas holidays and Pony Club championships, here we come!"

The championships were the last thing on Lily's mind. She was thinking of another idea, although it was tinged with guilt, seeing as it meant riding through the forest again without permission. She pushed that thought away – the unicorns came first. "Do you girls want to stay at my place tonight? Bring the ponies, then we can get back here easier tonight with Kuia's herbs and start our search earlier tomorrow?"

"I can stay. Great idea to get started as early as we can," Sasha said with a sigh. "Because I have to be home for a stupid family thing at two o'clock."

"I'll ask, Lily," said Chloe in her gentle voice. "I hope

Mum will let me stay. She's booked a maths tutor tomorrow afternoon, but she did say I could ride in the morning. I'll never be able to sneak out of home again tonight. I was frightened enough this morning."

Lily bit her lip. *I can't say it, but if that witch turns up, she is going to be way more frightening than Chloe's mother.*

Ambrosius spoke. "You're already coming back tonight to tend to Brökk, so you'll tell us what you've been able to find out then."

"If we bring a map, can we show you the options we find?" Chloe asked quietly. "Sorry if that sounds rude, but I don't know if you can read a map..." Her voice trailed off awkwardly.

"A valid question, Chloe," Ambrosius said kindly. "We are fortunate to have a special relationship with a trustworthy person in our homeland who keeps us up to date with the human world. We have even looked at internet pages about unicorns." He chuckled. "We find those most amusing."

Lily giggled at the idea. "So we could look at a map together and plan routes from this farm to possible hiding places?"

"Indeed we can," he replied. "Now you must go. Dawn is not far away."

Lily grabbed Rainbow's reins from Chloe. "Will you ride with us now, Sigvard? Then you'll know where to meet us tonight?"

The next second, she was galloping across the paddock beside the massive unicorn and her friends. For a moment, excitement overrode worry for the herd. *No one would ever believe this if you told them!*

. . .

Lily and Chloe saw Sasha pelting down her drive as the school bus pulled up outside. She was greeted with a chorus of "Nearly missed it!" from the other kids and a stern reminder to be on time next year from the driver.

Sasha swung into the seat behind them and leaned forward to whisper. "Did you get inside without anyone knowing, Chlo?"

Chloe twisted in her seat so they could whisper without being heard. "Mum was coming downstairs as I came in."

"Oh!" Lily looked at her friend, worried on her behalf. Mrs Cho was very strict.

"I said I'd been out for an early morning bike ride. That the piano teacher told me that physical exercise like horse riding and biking was important for mental clarity around the intensity of practising for the grading exams next year."

"Good thinking!" Sasha patted Chloe's shoulder.

Lily smiled. "Did she buy it?"

Chloe grinned. "She didn't even ask why I was wearing jodhpurs to ride my bike. She just walked into the kitchen and started adding more riding sessions to my weekly schedule for the holidays. As long as I can make most of them horse riding, not bike riding, that will be great. I'll get more time with you guys and the ponies! What about you, Sash?"

Sasha turned her face away to look out the window. "They were too busy fighting to notice me."

Lily reached around the seat to squeeze Sasha's hand. "I'm so sorry, Sash. That sounds horrible."

Their brave, confident friend sniffed hard, and her eyes were filled with tears when she looked back. "Yeah, it's really, really horrible. I don't know why they stay together if they make each other so miserable, but I don't want them to split up either. What would happen then?"

Lily glanced at Chloe, who looked as sad as she was feeling herself. What could she say? No one liked to hear that their friend's parents might divorce. Poor Sasha and her little sister Susie. She scooted around into Sasha's seat to hug her friend. "We'll be here for you. And you can come and stay any time you want if that helps."

Sasha wiped the tears out of her eyes. "Thanks, but I don't like to leave Dad alone with Mum too much. She and Susie are ganging up on him, and he needs someone to be on his side too."

Oh. How awful! She squeezed Sasha in another tight hug. "I hope something works out."

Sasha hugged her back. "I guess something will, somehow." Dropping her voice, meaning Chloe leaned further back over the seat to hear, she added, "Let's change the subject! How are we going to find *them* a hiding place?"

"I've been thinking..." Chloe started to reply as the bus pulled up outside school. They had to pile off with everyone else and head to class.

As they hung up their backpacks, Lily said: "As soon as the bell rings for break and lunchtime, I'm going to sprint for the library to bags a computer."

"Great. Try and get that one that faces the back wall," said Sasha. "We don't want people nosing into what we're looking at."

"It will only be maps and stuff," Chloe said. "No one will care."

Sasha plopped into a chair. "Not taking any chances."

Lily sat beside her, Chloe on the other side. "I'll get that computer if I can, but you know the geeky boys always try and get that one."

"Run faster then." Sasha lifted the desk lid to pull out her geography books.

"Morning, class!" Their teacher, Mrs Worthington, turned from the white-board where she'd been writing up today's lesson, and the chatter from their classmates lessened. "Quiet now. We're going to wrap up the year talking about sea caves and how they're formed. Seeing as Whale Bay is well-known for our sea caves, I'm sure you'll go into them again over summer, so now you'll be better informed."

Sasha leaned over. "Not made by a magical unicorn, I guess," she whispered.

"And if you're going to talk all day, Sasha Graham," said Mrs Worthington, "I'll move you away from your friends."

Sasha straightened in her chair. "Sorry, Mrs Worthington."

"Good." The teacher flicked on the big screen that replicated her computer screen. "These are the sea caves at Cathedral Cove on the east coast of the North Island, which are similar to ours in Whale Bay."

Mrs Worthington talked for some time. Lily's mind drifted. She wondered about how Ambrosius told them Brökk could make a chasm under the sea. How was that even possible? Before she knew it, her fingers held a pencil sketching the herd's most magical unicorn on a new page in her geography book.

Lost in trying to capture his eyes properly, she didn't notice the teacher standing behind her until Mrs Worthington cleared her throat.

"A unicorn, Lily? Not the questions from the white-board you're meant to be answering about sea caves."

Lily slapped her hand over the drawing. What was she thinking, drawing one of the supposedly secret unicorns? "Um, sorry, Mrs Worthington." What could she say? "I've been thinking of a story I want to write over the holidays."

"Really?" said the teacher. "I know it's the last day of

term, but some attention to this current lesson and not something better suited to creative writing classes would be appreciated."

"Yes, Mrs Worthington. Sorry." Lily turned to a blank page and looked intently at the questions on the board. She wrote number one then a dash, trying to focus on a sensible answer when she realised the teacher was still standing behind her.

"You're lucky there's no detention today, Lily, this being the final day of term."

Then, finally, the teacher walked away, leaving Lily frozen in shock. Imagine being sent to detention on the last day of the year! She had so much to do too. Train Rainbow. Tidy her room to fit the camp stretchers in for the girls. Help Mum with some chores to make up for the extra work of feeding her friends – that was the rule her parents had put in place a while ago as it always seemed to be Sasha and Chloe coming to stay at their house, not the other way around. Her parents welcomed Lily's friends but wanted Lily to understand it involved extra work.

She didn't mind. She usually enjoyed the chores like cleaning the working dogs' kennels and feeding them, sweeping the barn, picking vegetables from the garden and helping make dinner. Cleaning the hen house was the worst one – it was so smelly – but she liked seeing the hens happy, clucking among clean shavings, so that was okay too.

Oh, and Kuia wanted her to help sort the leaves they'd picked this morning not long after she'd got back from the unicorns. *Lucky Kuia didn't ask where we'd been riding so early. I couldn't have said we went through the forest in case she told Mum!*

She answered the white-board questions and was one of several people Mrs Worthington asked to read out their answers. The teacher simply said 'fine' and moved onto the next person, so she guessed her answers were okay.

The lesson dragged on, and all Lily wanted to hear was the bell. But when it came, she was thinking about Brökk and how they could help him get better faster.

Sasha nudged her. "The bell. Run! We'll bring your bag."

Shoot...!

She ran.

CHAPTER FIVE

L ily reached the library door at the same time as the geeky boys from their class. They were huddled over a hand-held screen, so she slipped in front of them and sprinted down the library aisle.

"No running!" ordered the librarian.

She slowed and glanced back. The geeks were behind, not far, so she walked as fast as she could to reach the seat at the computer that Sasha wanted.

She sat, her breath still coming fast, and looked around. Chloe and Sasha were just coming in the door as the boys reached Lily.

"Hey, we sit there," one of them said.

"Well, we're sitting here today."

"Yeah," said Sasha as the girls walked up. "It's not like there's a rule that only you can sit here."

The boy looked perplexed. "But...but we always do."

"Not today." Lily wasn't shifting. "Bring over another chair, Chloe, and let's get started."

Sasha put their backpacks under the desk and stood, arms folded, looking at the boy. "Well?"

"Never mind." He turned away, muttering with his friends.

"Finally." Sasha pulled up another chair so the three of them crowded around the computer screen.

Lily opened an internet browser, then pushed the keyboard and mouse over to Chloe. "Have you thought what websites might be good to look for parks on?" She kept the question quiet just in case someone was listening. Not that anyone else would know what they were talking about. But she'd rather not take any risks after the unicorn drawing in class. *That was stupid.*

"Of course." Chloe's fingers tapped quickly, and the first site flashed up. Whale Bay District Council. She searched for parks and a big list appeared.

"Do we have to click on each one to bring it up on a map?" Sasha asked, as she grabbed a book and pen out of her bag. "Or do you think there's a map of all the parks?"

"I'll keep this list open and look for a map on another page, so we can reference back easily." Chloe moved the cursor around the map on the screen to point out things they knew. "There's school. Wow, that's a really big park over behind it, eh?"

"I'll note that one," said Sasha. "What's the road name? We need to make sure it's got enough trees for the uni–"

"Ahem." Lily looked at Sasha and shook her head.

She looked sheepish and continued in a whisper. "For *you know who* to take cover during the day."

Chloe flicked between the two webpages, looking for the biggest parks first. The girls soon had a list of places they thought worth checking tomorrow. Then the first bell after break rang.

"Already!" Lily pushed back from the desk and put her

chair away. "There's more of the park map to work through."

"We'll have to do it tonight," replied Chloe. "Do you think we'll be allowed to use the computer at your place?"

"We should be, but it's right there in the dining room so Mum can see what I'm doing."

They walked out of the library and turned towards their class.

"Man, I'm hungry. I forgot we couldn't eat in the library." Sasha stuffed a sandwich in her mouth as they walked.

"Me too." Lily started on her lunch.

Chloe nibbled on an apple. "Perhaps if I did more searching and notes, while you two are helping your mum make dinner or something, then it doesn't look like a big deal."

"Good idea," Sasha replied. "Now we just have to get through one last afternoon with Mrs Worthington without getting into trouble. They talk about kids being grumpy at the end of the school year. Man, what about the teachers?" She looked at Lily, then whispered. "Tomorrow we'll be free to help the herd."

Lily grinned and pushed the classroom door open. "And train for the Pony Club champs!"

"See you a bit later!" Lily waved to Chloe as she jumped off the school bus. She pelted down the drive. She wanted all her chores done before the girls came over so there would be time for some training with the ponies before dinner as well as finishing the computer search. And then they had to get out to see the unicorns after dark without Mum and Dad knowing. The thought made her misjudge a step, and she nearly tripped over.

How long is it going to take us to find the herd a suitable hiding place? We can't keep sneaking out at night forever.

Sky came racing to Lily, tongue out, happy to see her. She patted his black and white head as they ran, panting, in the back door.

"Hi, Mum. Hi, Kuia."

They were at the dining table, having afternoon tea with Liam. Her little brother looked kind of sticky. Gross.

Lily put her backpack on its hook and her lunch box in the dishwasher. "I'm going to go sweep the barn and pick up muck in the yard and arena before I come in to help you, Kuia. Then I'll have a ride with Sasha and Chloe when they get here. Anything else, Mum?"

"Hello, my busy daughter." Mum got up and plopped a kiss on Lily's head. "Collect the eggs, please. Liam and I didn't get to that today. Did you decide what you're going to do with Rainbow's training?"

"I'm going back through the basics." Avoiding Liam's mucky, grabbing hands, Lily hugged Kuia, then took a blueberry muffin from the plate on the table. Through a mouthful, she added, "I really want to make sure I didn't skip a step somewhere."

"Good for you," said Mum, coming back with a facecloth.

"She's very independent, isn't she?" Kuia started clearing the table while Mum tried to clean the wriggling toddler. Lily took the last muffin on the plate as Kuia picked it up.

"Yes, she is, Ma. But that's how John and I want her to be. Resourceful and logical in her thinking."

"I'm going now, so don't worry about talking about me

behind my back," Lily said with a smile to her mother, one hand on the door handle, the other with an apple to share with Rainbow. "I've heard it all before!"

"Dinner at six thirty!" Mum called as Lily went out.

"Got that!" she yelled. "Come on, Sky! Race you down to the yards."

Lily closed her bedroom door. "I'm so tired!"

"And we've still got to go and see the unicorns." Sasha whispered as she stretched out on her camp bed.

"I know!" Lily whispered back.

It had been interesting working with Kuia to make the tonic, but oh, how her grandmother liked to talk. Lily had tried to listen and learn the different plants and why you picked each one at certain times of the year, but there was a lot to remember. When she asked about a tonic for a friend's pony who had been burnt, Kuia wanted to know how such a thing could happen. Lily didn't know what to say at first, then came up with something about an electric fence gone wrong. Kuia talked for a while about why people even needed things like electric fences, especially around horses, but did pull some other herbs out of her kit and make a tonic for Lily to give her 'friend'. She also gave Lily two herbal salves – one for burns and one for bruises – that she said could be smoothed directly onto the skin.

Lily had to run to get all her chores done before the girls arrived on their ponies with overnight things in their backpacks and halters over the ponies' bridles.

They managed to fit in about an hour's riding in Kahurangi's paddock, the one with rolling hills next to Rainbow and Gracie's big paddock, where Lily's dad had built several cross-country jumps from logs and banks. Lily watched her friends for a while as she made sure Rainbow was thoroughly warmed up with lots of trot and canter circles. High-spirited Tommy was giving Sasha some trouble before she cantered him fast up the hill a few times, while Chloe and her pretty Palomino steadily worked their way around the jumps in their usual calm way. Then Lily popped Rainbow over all the small jumps, concentrating on galloping fast between the jumps and collecting her pony in preparation for the next jump. He behaved perfectly, although young Kahurangi found it all very exciting and cantered around, her tail high, dashing to race beside one pony, then another. Sasha commented how much better she looked already. Lily agreed. Her mother was working miracles with the filly, who was also getting Kuia's tonic.

When they came in, Lily and Sasha made sure to help Lily's mother get dinner ready while Chloe said she was finishing a project, and could she please research some things on the computer.

Dinner had been awkward, especially when Lily's mum asked after the girls' families.

Sasha stared at her plate, silent for some time, before looking up and saying baldly that she thought her parents were going to get a divorce.

"Oh," said Lily's mum. "I'm very sorry to hear that. Please tell your mother that you and Susie are welcome to stay here anytime if they need some time to talk. Actually, I'll phone her tomorrow."

Sasha's cheeks flushed red as she stared down again.

Oh, maybe that wasn't the right thing for Mum to say.

Thankfully her mother noticed Sasha wasn't happy and asked if Sasha would rather she didn't phone.

Sasha swallowed. "Please don't." Her voice was quiet. "Mum doesn't want people to know. Well, she's telling all her friends about how awful Dad is and stuff, when he isn't, but I don't think she wants me to tell anyone."

Kuia was sitting beside Sasha and leaned over to wrap Sasha in a hug. Lily was even sadder for her friend when she saw a tear plop onto the tablecloth.

"Poor little mokopuna," Kuia said, with her cheek against Sasha's hair. "You come see Tessa, John and me anytime you need a hug, eh? All children, they need lots of hugs, especially at sad times."

Looking at Sasha now, lying on the camp bed, Lily wondered if she was right to have asked Sasha to help with the search for the unicorn's hiding place.

"You alright, Sash?" Lily asked quietly as Chloe came in from the bathroom.

"I guess." Sasha looked at Lily for a second, then away to the wall.

"Are you okay about going to see the unicorns tonight?"

Sasha's blond head flicked back. "Yes!" She sat up. "Why would you ask that?"

"Chloe and I are worried about you."

Chloe nodded. "Things don't sound good at home."

"They're not." Sasha sat cross-legged. "But don't tell me to stay away from the unicorns because of that... They're the best thing that's happened all year!"

Lily smiled. "If you're sure."

"One hundred per cent sure." Sasha wriggled down in her sleeping bag. "Now, switch that light off so we can get some sleep before the alarm wakes us up again!"

The house was dark and quiet when Lily slipped her backpack on, her computer tablet and the bottles of herbal tonic padded safely inside it. She twisted the handle of her door to ease it open. Fumbling, she found Chloe's hand and hoped Chloe had hold of Sasha's hand as they'd discussed. Placing each foot carefully, she padded through the house leading her friends.

Quack!

Lily leapt sideways and nearly crashed into the wall, only Chloe's hand holding her upright. She clapped her other hand over her mouth in fright.

"What was that?" Sasha hissed.

"Dog toy," whispered Lily. She took a breath to calm her nerves and listened. No sound except their breathing. Pushing the toy well out of the way, she tugged Chloe's hand to continue. *I've got to pick up everything that might be in our way before we go to bed.*

Outside, the moon was a fraction larger than last night and already up over the horizon, turning everything silver. Breathing out in relief that step one was complete, Lily put her finger to her lips. They mustn't talk until they were well away from the house.

Safely at the barn, Lily said quietly, "Close the door carefully before we turn the light on."

"Even better," replied Sasha, "open it wide to let the moonlight in and don't turn the light on at all so we don't lose our night vision."

"Good idea. But try not to let stirrup irons clink on buckles."

Chloe whispered, "Don't forget the collapsible bucket to give Brökk the tonic."

She fumbled in the darkest corner to find the canvas bucket they used for shows and a bit of twine to tie it to her saddle. A few minutes later they were all outside, holding their tack, and she was able to safely close the barn. Another step done.

It's harder sneaking out tonight than this morning. At least in the morning, if Mum and Dad heard anything outside, they might think it's a neighbour getting up early. But night-time is so quiet with everyone in bed and animals resting.

The ponies were surprised to see them, looking up from where they were grazing with Gracie.

"Lucky Tommy and Angel like your horses and they're all together," Sasha said quietly as she fished a carrot out of her jodhpurs' pocket for Tommy, who wasn't always easy to catch.

"Sure is." Lily ran her hand down Rainbow's neck before slipping the reins over his head. "Here, I'll hold all the ponies while you two put your saddles on."

Seconds later, all ponies were tacked up. Lily held the restless Tommy while Sasha mounted, then swung up onto Rainbow. They set off across the silvery grass, the constant scent of sea and native bush surrounding them. She breathed deeply. How she loved the smells of home.

"Do you think Sigvard will be there?" Sasha asked eagerly, riding out in front.

"He said he would be at the gate from moonrise." Chloe said.

"He did, Chlo." Lily looked at her gentle, easily frightened friend riding alongside. "Are you okay?"

"I'm almost more nervous than this morning, which doesn't make sense."

"I feel the same. It's weird, eh?"

"This morning it was all new, so excitement overrode the nerves," replied Chloe with her usual logical thought. "Now I've been through the forest in the dark, I keep thinking of all the things that can go wrong. If one of the ponies spikes itself on those jagged broken bits of pine tree, it would be out of the qualifying competition. If the gates are locked and we have to jump in the dark. And I don't want to think what could happen if Abellona reaches Whale Bay before the unicorns can find a better hiding place."

With each of Chloe's statements, Lily felt more anxious. The very thought of the witch terrified her too, but mostly for the unicorns. The worst was the idea of Ambrosius and Sigvard being forced to fight under Abellona's control against other unicorns. That she couldn't bear.

"Come on, you two worrywarts," Sasha said, cutting through Lily's swirling thoughts. "We've got more unicorns to meet, and Brökk needs that tonic, right? Let's trot."

Lily let Rainbow trot with the other ponies. *Sasha is right. I do want to help Brökk and meet all the foals. I just hope Abellona is still a long way away.*

"He's there!" As soon as Sasha saw Sigvard, she pushed Tommy into a canter. The next second she'd slipped from the saddle, scrambled over the gate and rushed to Sigvard. He lowered his head, that ivory spike swinging dangerously close to Lily's impulsive friend.

Lily froze. "Sasha, be careful!" Sigvard had been looking at Sasha a lot this morning, but she didn't know if that was a good thing or not.

Sasha dodged the swing of Sigvard's head and flung her arms as far as she could reach around his huge neck. She turned, her eyes shining with happy tears. "Oh, Lil, I don't know how you kept the unicorns a secret from us for one second last night."

Sigvard lowered his head and nibbled Sasha's blond ponytail, making her giggle.

"Lily, look," Chloe whispered beside her.

The huge unicorn seemed to sigh and relax as their

friend ran her hands over his dark, dappled grey head. He closed his eyes and rested his muzzle on her shoulder.

Wow. He likes Sasha. A lot.

"Is that what it's like for you and Ambrosius?" Chloe asked quietly.

"Yes, but how did you know? I didn't say anything." The feeling Lily had with Ambrosius was kind of private, and she hadn't felt like talking about it with her friends.

"I watched you, Lily, that's all." Chloe smiled in the moonlight. "Maybe you'll tell me about it later, but we better get going. Who knows how long we'll be tonight, and we've got to get some sleep or we won't be able to search in the morning."

"You're right." She nudged Rainbow forward. "Um, Sasha, Sigvard, we need to get to the herd."

The unicorn's eyes flashed open and Sasha stumbled as she stepped away. She looked kind of dazed but didn't say anything as she unlatched the gate to let the ponies through.

"Come," said Sigvard. "Ambrosius awaits."

Sigvard walked off along the track, his dark grey dappled coat lost in the intense darkness among the pine forest. Sasha and Tommy were right beside him. "Come on, guys," she called.

"It's very dark, Sasha." Lily nudged Rainbow forward, Chloe and Angel alongside. She could hardly see her own hands on the reins, let alone where her pony was walking.

"Sigvard, turn your glow on," Sasha instructed the most warrior-like of the unicorns. "That's why you came to meet us, remember?"

Sigvard paused. "You're right, my apologies." Around him a warm light grew, pushing back the shadows. "I'm not feeling quite myself."

Sasha and her chestnut gelding shone brightly in the

pool of light as they walked up the forestry track. "I forgot how cool this is!"

Lily couldn't work out the look that Sigvard gave Sasha. Kind of confused, perhaps.

He replied. "Let us move faster. The night will pass more swiftly than you realise." With that, he broke into a canter. Slow, Lily thought, by his standards, but plenty fast enough for the ponies on a rough track. Not that Rainbow seemed to mind; he was full of energy and needed checking from time to time through the ups and downs of the forestry track.

Sigvard made an easy leap over the boundary gate while Sasha unlatched the gate for the ponies. "You could have come through the gate with us, Sigvard," she said.

"But why?" his deep voice rumbled with humour. "It barely comes up to my elbow."

Sasha laughed as they cantered along the grass verge, which they could see easily thanks to Sigvard's circle of light. They swept around into the driveway of the abandoned farm. Sigvard called a halt as they crested the drive and, breathing hard, the ponies pulled up beside the King's lieutenant.

CHAPTER SIX

"Oh. My. God," Sasha breathed. "I forgot how beautiful they are."

Lily drank in the sight of the unicorn herd dotted around the wide pasture. Each unicorn was bathed in its own nimbus of light, and where a pair grazed side by side, the pools of light merged to be bigger and brighter.

Magical and magnificent. She sighed. *Like the most beautiful horses you've ever seen, with one difference – they all have that steely glint of a unicorn horn.*

"Wow." Chloe sighed. "It's amazing to see them like this, isn't it?"

Lily could only nod, her heart full of an unexpected love for the whole herd.

"I love all the colours," Chloe continued, her voice hushed. "Some like Sigvard, that deep, burnished pewter grey. Look, those ones are almost pure white – I wonder if they're very old. There's every shade of dappled silver-grey, some with dark manes, some with lighter manes. And the foals, of course, which are much darker. Kind of like Lipizzaner horses, aren't they, in that way?"

"Yes," replied Lily, knowing Chloe referred to the breed of white horses who were born black, made famous by the Spanish Riding School of Vienna. She'd studied their history for a school project. "Do you see how they have very small horns, like they're just starting to grow?"

The foals were absolutely darling.

And that made her even more worried.

Ambrosius's request for them to help hide the herd from Abellona felt very real as she watched a foal suckling from its mother. What if they tried their very best but still couldn't help the unicorns?

She took a deep breath and tried to let the worry go. Like Kuia always said, worrying doesn't change anything, except make you more worried.

Sigvard's voice interrupted her thoughts. "Come. Ambrosius is with Brökk."

Reaching the pair, Ambrosius greeted them warmly. "I am pleased to see you all. Forgive my eagerness, but I hope your internet search was fruitful."

The unicorn's friendly welcome made Lily feel a bit better. *He trusts us to help as best we can, and that's what we're doing.* "We have some possibilities." She dismounted, looped and buckled Rainbow's reins around his neck so they wouldn't slip off over his head, and ran the stirrups up the leathers before letting him go to graze. "Don't go far, Rainbow."

"He won't," said Ambrosius.

"How do you know?" Lily asked, slipping her backpack off as the others dismounted and did the same with their ponies.

"I asked him, and he said so."

She stopped. "You asked him? How?"

"Any one of us – even a foal – can communicate with

your ponies." The unicorn king chuckled. "We are all equines after all."

"Well, please ask Tommy not to be difficult being caught again," Sasha said as she patted her chestnut pony and let him go.

Sigvard snorted with amusement. "He says he thinks it's funny to make you run."

"Oh, does he?" Sasha tried not to smile but failed. "You're very cheeky, Tommy!"

The pony lifted his tail and farted as he trotted off.

"He knows what I said!" Laughing, Sasha turned to Sigvard.

"Horses understand a lot more than humans believe," the warrior unicorn replied. "And now, to your search."

"I know, but Brökk first if that's okay," Lily replied, reaching into her backpack. "Chloe, do you want to start the tablet? And Sasha, could you get the bucket off Rainbow's saddle and half fill it with water from the trough, please?"

She pulled out the tonic and walked beside Ambrosius to where the darkest of all the unicorns had moved to lie down under a tree.

Lily sensed a kind of hum, a buzz of energy around Brökk. *If I can feel this now, imagine what it's like when he's healthy and strong.*

"My friend," Ambrosius said to the mage, "you remember Lily."

Brökk lifted his head with a sigh. "Greetings, young one." His voice croaked with exhaustion.

Lily knelt beside the unicorn mage and stroked his neck. Her hand warmed as the feeling of immense power intensified. "It's good to see you, Brökk. I hope you're feeling a little better tonight." Was it really only twenty-four hours since she'd first seen the unicorns?

"Ja, a little better, but not out of danger!" He sounded upset, and the hum of magical power fractured for a moment. "No, we are all still very much in danger. So much so that we need to risk asking for help from a human we do not know in a land unfamiliar to us. Bah!" Brökk looked away into the trees with a snort of disgust.

Lily sat back on her heels. *What can I say that doesn't upset him more? If you look at it from Brökk's point of view, he's right – they are still in danger. But at least they escaped Abellona for the time being. He did the best that he could, and now he's exhausted and hurt.*

"Brökk, if you don't mind," she said respectfully, "I have bought the herbal tonic we talked about this morning."

"Well, other than time to rest, which we don't have, or being able to cast a strengthening spell upon myself, which I don't have the strength to do, we don't seem to have any option other than to try your tonic, do we?"

Oh dear. Lily looked at Ambrosius. Was she making things worse?

"Now, Brökk, there's no need to put your frustrations on Lily," Ambrosius said gently. "She's just trying to help, and you must admit, we need all the help we can get right now."

Brökk looked away into the distance for a long while as Lily waited anxiously. Then he sighed loudly, his head bowed down to the ground. "Very true, Sire. I apologise. That was uncalled for."

After a slow breath, he looked at Lily, his eyes showing some of the spark that she imagined was more usual. "Bring forth your tonic," he said politely.

Carrying the bucket, Sasha crouched down beside Lily, who opened the small bottle. "My grandmother is a respected healer in the old traditions of the Māori people. She said this will help heal your burns."

Brökk looked towards Ambrosius, who nodded his encouragement. "It's worth trying, Brökk, is it not? We have herbalists in our country after all."

The mage sniffed at the bottle. "It doesn't smell dangerous anyway."

Lily smiled. "This is rongoā – Māori medicine – used for hundreds, if not thousands of years."

Carefully, using the unicorn light, she measured out two capfuls and swished it around in the water.

"If you would like to drink this bucket slowly over the next half hour, my grandmother says that's best. I'll leave another one made up for you for the morning."

Brökk took a cautious sip. "Ja, I will do that."

"The grass here is good for grazing, Ambrosius," said Sasha, "but is Brökk able to eat? Would some other kind of food be helpful?"

"How do you mean, child?"

"Like the hard feed we have for the ponies. High nutrition horse pellets made from grain."

"Oh, that's a good idea, Sasha," Chloe chipped in. "What a shame we didn't think of that before we came over tonight."

"We are familiar with it. If you wish to return tomorrow, I'm sure the additional food will be very welcome," Ambrosius said. "I can think of a few of foals who could also benefit. Perhaps we can see them once we look at your map."

"We'd love to," Lily smiled. "When Brökk is finished, we could give the foals a little tonic as well. I have one for exhaustion and stress too."

"If you feel it will help them, by all means."

Happiness surged through Lily. She didn't know much about Kuia's herbs – yet – but it felt good to help.

Lily got to her feet, unsure how the grumpy, injured

mage would react to her next suggestion. She swallowed. "Um, Brökk, do you think I could check you over...? I have two salves, balms, from my grandmother, one for burns, one for cuts and bruises. We know you have burns and perhaps other injuries I can treat. Are you able to stand up for a few minutes, please?"

She thought she heard Brökk groan.

"Only if it's not too painful," she added.

"Are you able, Brökk?" Ambrosius asked gently.

With a sigh and several more groans, the mage stood up. He shook his head carefully, then looked at Lily. "All right, get on with it."

"I'll try not to hurt you." Gently, she ran her hands down Brökk's shoulder, feeling for heat which indicated bruising or cuts on a horse and, presumably, a unicorn.

Avoiding his legs for the moment, as she knew they were burnt, Lily felt something on his chest. She looked hard, struggling to make it out against his black coat. "It looks like another burn."

"Ja, burns everywhere, like we already said. I'm often burned making chasms," he grumbled. "But usually I can fix them myself."

"Can I put the salve on?"

"If you do my legs as well."

Pleased he was accepting her help, Lily gently applied the salve. Sasha and Chloe gently stroked Brökk's head and neck. Bit by bit, Lily could feel him relax.

Perhaps he's never had much contact with the person Ambrosius talked about. Maybe we're the first people to touch him.

That was a nice feeling.

"Brökk, why didn't tell us you were so badly burnt?" Chloe's question was quiet.

The mage was silent for some time. "I didn't agree with Ambrosius that three small human girls could help us."

Oh. Lily hesitated, then Sasha asked the question before she could.

"So why do you trust us to help you now?"

Brökk sighed as Lily crouched down to apply the burn salve to his fetlocks. "I must be honest and say I questioned Ambrosius when he rushed straight into this connection with Lily. That was not wise. But to find a believer right away, things did seem to be going in our favour. Perhaps you will be able to help us keep out of Abellona's clutches."

Lily bit her lip. "I didn't know if I could help, but I think I am – I mean, we are, aren't we?"

"Indeed, you are." Ambrosius nuzzled her shoulder.

Brökk replied, "I no longer doubt you are doing everything you can to help, Lily. I can feel the salve working already." Tears sprung in Lily's eyes at his sudden praise of her efforts. "It seems our Sire was right to trust his instincts when he felt the strength of the connection with you."

Wow. Lily kept her head down, blinking the tears away as she finished soothing the rich herbal balm on Brökk's leg.

Chloe's quiet voice came next. "If you don't mind me asking, have you never felt a connection with a human, Brökk?"

"I have not. Perhaps I have been too cautious. I have always felt I must protect my powers, and from my observations, one can never be sure how that connection with a human may result."

Lily stood up, screwing the lid on the jar. "A connection might not be a positive thing?"

"Not always," replied Ambrosius. Lily wondered what happened for him to say that.

"Oh, that's interesting," said Sasha, her hands tidying Sigvard's curly mane where she could reach.

"We'll talk about it sometime," said Ambrosius, "but now I want to see what possibilities for another location you have found."

Lily wiped her hands on the grass. "Let's look at that webpage Chloe bookmarked. Can you show us, Chlo?"

Chloe turned so the unicorns could look over her shoulder at the map open on the little screen. "Right, so we're here now." She pointed out the dead-end of Sanderson Road and the abandoned farm. "There's the forest behind us. Lily said you came up from the beach here."

Lily spoke. "Looking at the first possibility we found near school, which is possibly large enough, it would mean a long way by road." She leaned in to trace her finger along a route from the abandoned farm onto the main highway then around the back of town to a park near their school.

She frowned. "We're worried how the whole herd could travel unseen along the highway."

"Hmm." Ambrosius nodded.

"The problem is that nearly all the parks we found would have a similar route." Chloe tapped the screen to show four other options.

"Yes, we see that," said Sigvard.

Ambrosius said, "We can send Guilio to scout ahead, but he is only one pegasus and also in danger of being seen."

Lily chewed her lip, worried. "I don't know how you'd get to any of these without being seen, but we plan to ride around as many of the parks as we can tomorrow morning to see how near houses they are, whether there are good hiding places, access to fresh water. How much grazing do you need?"

"We have fifty mares, fifteen with foals at foot and thirty warriors," replied Sigvard.

"So that's nearly one hundred all together," came Chloe's quick response.

"How do you add so quickly?" Lily flashed a smile at her friend, who always topped the maths tests. "That's a lot of grazing. I didn't think to count when we saw you this morning. Some of those parks will be too small." She paused to think. "Are you sure you can't stay where you are until Brökk is well again? I can't see how all of you can safely travel along the main highway anyway – there's always trucks no matter what the time of night."

"Every day we stay within a day's travel of the chasm is another day closer Abellona is likely to be."

"A day's travel?" Lily looked at Ambrosius, concerned. "But none of these parks are that far away."

"But if they're close enough to humans so that human scent helps disguise us, that will definitely help."

"O-k-a-y," she said slowly, still concerned they'd been looking for the wrong sort of hiding place.

Chloe asked, "How many days does it take you to come through the chasm?"

"Without the passing of day and night, it's difficult to be accurate, but approximately three," said Sigvard.

"You must all have been very tired." Lily smoothed her hand down Ambrosius's muzzle.

"We were, especially the mares and foals, despite setting our pace to look after the youngest as best we could," he replied.

"You talked about a distraction, right?" Chloe continued. "So that gave you a head-start on Abellona?"

"Ja, we waited to leave until Guilio could barely sense his brother's presence, which meant Galen and therefore

Abellona, who was following Pudersnö, were on the far side of our land."

"How would she know you'd left? And if she's had to track your departure point and travel through the chasm, she might be days away." Chloe's voice lifted with hope.

"We anticipate she would know within hours of our departure," replied Sigvard. "Although we managed to stay hidden from Abellona for many months, the sheer force of magic that Brökk had to exert to create the chasm would immediately be noticed. One of her many spies would undoubtedly have passed on that information."

"She sounds horrible!" Lily's stomach was queasy. Imagine living in hiding and a witch so evil she'd force you to fight in her private army.

Ambrosius sighed. "That is the way it has been for many years."

"We've chanced our lives by coming to your country." Sigvard's voice was dark. "Yet it is a gamble we would make again if we can change our future."

"We've got to be able to help," Sasha said with passion. "Somehow!"

"We already are," said Chloe decisively. "Let's focus on finding the best hiding place we can. How long do you think it would take Abellona to reach the chasm?"

"About three days, maybe less," replied Ambrosius.

"Okay, so if you arrived last night, Thursday, after about three days in the chasm, she could have entered it as you emerged, right?"

Lily saw Chloe's logic and nodded, as Sigvard replied snappily, "Yes, we know that."

"Well, I'm just trying to make sure we all understand correctly," Chloe replied with an authority that surprised

Lily for her normally soft-spoken friend. "It's Friday night now, so we have only forty-eight hours."

"So they have to move by Sunday night?" Lily asked to be certain she followed the timeline.

"That's right. The other problem I see is if there's nothing around Whale Bay that could work as a hiding place, it's a long way to another town and other people. And we wouldn't be able to get there to check things anyway. You'd just have to leave here and travel through the big native forest which wraps right round Whale Bay and hope you get far enough away from the chasm that Abellona has trouble finding you."

Ambrosius spoke. "Which offers Brökk little opportunity to rest."

Chloe nodded.

If Lily felt sick before, she felt even worse now. If they couldn't find a big enough park tomorrow, where would the unicorns go?

"Then let's find somewhere!" Sasha hugged Sigvard's neck again. "We have to!"

CHAPTER SEVEN

They leaned over the little tablet screen again, retracing roads to the different parks and discussing pros and cons.

The largest one looked most promising, but it was way over the other side of the main highway. It would take too long to get there on the ponies in the time Sasha and Chloe had available tomorrow morning, so they decided to check the biggest parks closest to town. Until they looked at them properly, they couldn't be sure if there were trees to hide amongst or enough grazing to support the herd for a few days.

"We're going to have to move again eventually," Ambrosius said. "We just need this place to rest safely until Brökk has healed."

"I wish we could get to that big park though," Lily said again.

"We'll look at it online tonight," Chloe said. "That might be enough."

Sasha yawned. "Thank goodness we've decided where we're going in the morning, although how we're going to stay awake to ride home tonight let alone do this search, I have no idea."

"Forgive me for not thinking of this earlier. My mind has been otherwise occupied," said Ambrosius. "Lily, Sasha, Chloe, step close to me and turn up your faces."

He shook his long, silver mane and a pearly dust covered the girls.

Sasha giggled. "It tickles!"

Lily licked the pearly coating off her lips. "Oh, it's kind of sweet and really yummy." She smiled seeing her friends' faces luminescent in the moonlight. Realising she must look the same, she laughed with Sasha.

"And how do you feel?" he asked.

"Wide awake, like I could stay up all night," replied Lily.

"Wow, yeah, not at all tired," Sasha added. "What if we want to sleep?"

Ambrosius chuckled. "You'll be able to stay awake when you want to and sleep soundly when you want to."

"That's magic!" Sasha said.

Everyone laughed. Then she realised what she'd said and joined in.

"And there's something else." Ambrosius touched his muzzle to Sasha's head. "It appears we have another believer in you, beautiful Sasha, if what Sigvard tells me of your connection is true."

The muscular unicorn nodded as Sasha looked up at Ambrosius, her mouth open. "Is that what it is?" Her voice trembled. "Like Sigvard is the most important thing in the whole wide world?" She rushed to wrap her arms around Sigvard's neck.

"It must be true, Sire." Sigvard's normally clipped voice

was filled with emotion. "It's the first time I've felt the connection with a human."

"Ah," said Ambrosius with meaning. "It's rather special, is it not?"

Sigvard nodded his head again as much as Sasha's arms would allow. "Very special."

Lily looked from Sasha and Sigvard to Ambrosius. "Could you ever have imagined that two of us would have this special connection? I mean why us?"

"I have no idea why, Lily," Ambrosius said in his deep voice. "Perhaps one of the ancients would know. But they have not been among us for many years. It's never happened in our herd, I can tell you that much. But let us focus on practical things. The night is passing, and we are conscious you need to return. Shall we tend to some of the weaker foals before you depart?"

"I'll just get the bucket and some more water." Lily walked back to Brökk, who appeared to be sleeping. *The bucket's empty, so that's good.* She refilled it and came back to the others.

"Oh, come on, Sigvard," Sasha was saying. "Take me for a ride around the paddock."

The king's lieutenant replied with a loud snort, making Chloe jump and drop the tablet.

"Where's your backpack, Lil?" she asked. "I'll put this away and carry it seeing as you've got the bucket."

Lily handed it to Chloe and laughed at Sasha wiping unicorn snot off her jacket. "That sounds like a no, Sash."

"Yuck," she replied with feeling. "I guess it is, but one day, I am going to ride him."

Sigvard snorted again and pranced off.

Lily laughed. "No offence, but I think Sigvard's the one to make that decision."

Still amazed at her friend's determination to *ride a unicorn*, Lily walked with the others to a mare and a foal under some trees at the top of a steep gully. *I don't know if I could ever ask Ambrosius that. He's too magnificent to have a human ride him. Maybe the good witch Celestina could ride him or Sigvard. Or perhaps she rides Guilio like her evil sister rides Guilio's brother Galen. But with his permission, not like Abellona rides Galen because she forces him.*

Ambrosius' voice bought Lily back to the present. "This is Eva and her colt Lief."

Lily held her hand out to the mare to sniff. "Is she okay with me touching her foal, Ambrosius?"

"You can ask Eva yourself, Lily. We can all speak to humans if we wish."

"It still doesn't seem possible." Lily let the foal sniff her hand. "You, the whole herd don't seem possible. I can't believe I only met you for the first time last night."

"This morning for Sasha and me." Chloe stroked Eva's neck. "Surreal is how I'm feeling, and now we're all glowing with magical unicorn dust!"

"I know, right? Totally surreal." The foal lipped Lily's hair. "I guess we're the first people he's ever seen."

"You are, but I told Lief not to be frightened," Ambrosius said.

"He's certainly not afraid," Lily smiled as she gently pushed Lief's nibbling teeth away from her jacket. "I'll check Lief for bruises and injuries now, if that's okay, Eva."

"Ja, of course," the mare replied calmly as Lily started running her hands down the foal's spindly legs. He was nearly as tall as Rainbow, yet still a baby.

"Can I help, Lil?" Chloe asked.

"Yes, please." Lily looked to where the unicorn king and

75

Sigvard were grazing the lush grass a few feet away. "How many foals do you want us to check, Ambrosius?"

"Five," he said, chewing hungrily.

"Sash, can you help too?" Lily measured out a half dose of the herbs and swished it into the bucket of water. "See if you can get Lief to drink a few mouthfuls, while Chloe and I apply salve to any hot areas."

Working together, the girls met four more mares and their foals, applying the salves for burns or bruises where needed and offering the restorative tonic.

Walking back across the rolling paddock to Brökk, Lily said, "I think Lief was the weakest, but he seemed a bit brighter even as we came back past him."

Ambrosius replied, "He is our youngest, so it's understandable the journey was most difficult for him."

"We'll bring that hard feed when we come back tomorrow night," Chloe added.

"Do you think that's soon enough?" Lily thought. "I could leave some in a bucket by the forest gate when we get back tonight. Could you carry a bucket handle in your mouth?"

"Of course. I will accompany you back through the forest anyway," said Sigvard, who had Sasha walking close beside him, her hand holding his mane. "Is it safe for me to come closer to where you keep this feed? Then I can bring it straight back tonight."

Sasha replied cheerfully, "If anyone in Lily's family is awake in the middle of the night and looking anywhere near the barn then we're all in trouble anyway."

Lily pulled a face at her friend. "You don't sound worried if we were seen. I don't even want to think about how much trouble we'd be in, being out at night like this."

"I got to meet Sigvard and all the others," Sasha

responded. "It's worth all the trouble I could get in at home."

"Easy for you to say," said Chloe as they approached Brökk. "Your mother isn't threatening to sell your pony if you don't pass your piano exams."

"Oh, Chlo," Lily rubbed her friend's shoulder. "That's awful. But you will pass, won't you? Because you're very good."

"I have to practice a lot."

"So keep practising and keep your pony," Sasha said in the blunt way she sometimes had.

"We'll be fine," Lily reassured her friend – and herself. "No one's going to see us, and Sigvard can come up to the barn with us. It's out of sight of the house."

Ambrosius rubbed his cheek on Lily's shoulder. "I apologise, Lily. By asking you to help us, we risk causing you problems at home."

Lily stopped, running her hand down the unicorn king's silvery face. "It's okay, Ambrosius. We choose to do this, to help you. We'll be fine," she repeated. And crossed her fingers as she slipped her hand back in her pocket.

They found Brökk standing up, grazing.

"Are you feeling a little better?" Ambrosius asked the mage.

"I do seem to have an appetite," Brökk replied between mouthfuls. "The grass here, it's delicious."

The king nodded. "Everyone is saying the same. You did well to bring us to this fertile land so far away from our own."

"Hmmm," replied Brökk, munching hard. "I'm glad I managed to direct the chasm to the coastline. It's not a very big land mass to find from under the ocean floor."

Lily and Chloe looked at each other, astonished to hear

Brökk nearly didn't find land safely. *What would have happened to the herd if he hadn't bought them up in the right place?*

"Now give me some more of that tonic, young Lily," the mage lifted his head. "I do believe it's helped a great deal."

Grinning with delight to see Brökk so improved, Lily ran to the trough to get more water. "Here you are." She swished the measure of tonic around.

"Excellent." He took a long drink. "Now Mikaela, where are you? You should have some too as I'm concerned your energies are depleted trying to boost mine."

A fine-boned, dappled grey mare came towards them.

"Ah, good," said Brökk. "Do drink up."

"He's like a different unicorn," Chloe whispered to Lily while Mikaela drank.

"I know," Lily whispered back. "He must heal up very quickly. Maybe it's the magic inside him."

"And isn't Mikaela beautiful? Do you think I could touch her?"

The mare lifted her head from the bucket, water dripping from her dark muzzle. "You only need to ask," she spoke directly to Chloe, who ducked her head shyly.

"Go on, Chlo." Lily nudged her.

Stumbling over a grass clump, Chloe nearly fell at Mikaela's feet. The unicorn dropped her head, giving Chloe a gentle push to help her stand upright.

"Oh!" Chloe leaned back. "That prickled."

"Not another one," Sigvard said with a groan. "Touch Mikaela properly."

Unsure, Chloe looked around. "What do you mean, another one?"

"If you feel a connection with Mikaela, that's three, isn't

it?" he replied. "Can you imagine the odds of this happening? You better touch her properly to be sure."

Chloe reached out her hand to Mikaela's cheek. "Oh, it's warm, really warm." The mare leaned into Chloe's touch. "There's that tingle again."

"Do you feel it, Mikaela?" Ambrosius asked.

"From what you've described previously, Sire, yes, I do," Mikaela replied in her velvety voice.

"Three girls, three connections." Sigvard sighed.

"And the problem is?" Ambrosius asked.

"You know things always get complicated when we have active human connections."

Sasha huffed in disbelief. "Gee, Sigvard, do you think your life wasn't complicated until you met us? What's not complicated about living in hiding from a mad witch or being captured to fight against your own kind, setting up diversions to avoid her and travelling through a magical portal to the other side of the world? And that's just the stuff you've told us. How did Celestina get captured and things like that? Was that complicated in any way?"

Lily was lost for words, listening to the way Sasha talked to Sigvard – although she agreed with what Sasha said.

Sigvard dipped his head in acknowledgement. "You make a valid point."

Sasha nodded, then hugged the unicorn's neck. "I'm sorry that things are so difficult for you all, Sigvard, but I'm not sorry that it brought you here to me. You're honestly the best thing that's ever happened to me."

The king's lieutenant huffed a deep breath over Sasha. "I do not know what will come of our connection, young one, but I find I cannot be sorry that we have had this opportunity."

Chloe was leaning against Mikaela's shoulder, her face pressed against the mare's silky coat. Her voice was muffled as she said, "Maybe we're a good kind of complication. Maybe there's some reason why Brökk brought you here to our part of New Zealand, to the beach where you met Lily, some reason we don't understand yet."

"I know you like things to be logical, Chlo," Lily said as she petted Ambrosius, "but I think you're right. This is one of those times when you just have to believe that things have happened for a reason even if we don't understand it."

Lily paused, letting the thought sink in. *It was all mind-blowing whichever way you looked at it – unicorns, them each having a connection to a special unicorn, finding a hiding place, the witch.* She took a deep breath. *Wow.*

"Anyway, it's time to get home now. Even though we don't feel tired, we've still got to sleep."

Chloe looked at her watch using Mikaela's glow. "Oh, it's after midnight. The ponies need a rest too."

"Then let's ask them to join us." Ambrosius raised his head and whinnied.

Rainbow, Tommy and Angel lifted their heads and looked.

"Come on," the unicorn king said quietly.

The three ponies trotted over to the group standing with Ambrosius.

"That's pretty cool, Ambrosius, thanks." Lily patted the unicorn's neck and then her well-behaved pony.

CHAPTER EIGHT

The ride home through the forest was taken gently seeing as the ponies had another long ride through town in just a few hours.

Trotting beside Chloe, behind Sasha and Sigvard, Lily asked a question she'd been thinking about for a while. "Sigvard, do you know if the pearly dust Ambrosius shook over us would work on the ponies? So they aren't tired either."

"I don't know, Lily. Perhaps he could try it tonight when you return."

"Okay. I'll ask him."

"Can you make the same magical dust, Sigvard?" Sasha asked.

"No, Sasha, I can't. It's something Ambrosius inherited from his mother who was a strong mage much like Brökk."

"So you can all make and control your light, but you can't do anything more magical?"

"That's right. I'm from warrior bloodlines and proud of it." He snorted as if to emphasise his words.

Lily was intrigued. "How did Ambrosius become king,

Sigvard? Is it some kind of fight like the stallions of a horse herd?"

"Not really, but it's a long story, Lily, and one that Ambrosius should tell you himself. But he became our leader fair and square, and I follow him as our Sire with pride and respect."

What does he mean? Why wouldn't it be fair that Ambrosius is the herd's king? Lily wondered how she and Ambrosius would ever have the time to ask and answer that sort of question.

"You know, the dust is still all over your face, Lil." Chloe's voice cut through her thoughts. "I guess it's all over mine too," Chloe continued. "How are we going to get it off so no one sees it? And how would you get it off the ponies?"

Lily rubbed her face, then looked at her hand. It glistened in Sigvard's light. "I wonder if it only works when it's on your skin, or now that it's been on my skin, it will keep working even if I rub it off."

"I think we need to try and rub it off anyway or it's just going to end up on our pillows and clothes. Mum would not be happy to find it." Chloe scrubbed at her face.

"No, nor would my mum." Lily rubbed her forehead, and her hand was covered in the pearly powder. "Oh, heck." She rubbed it on her jodhpurs, which then glimmered just as much. "Oh, that's worse!"

Sasha looked back from where she was riding beside Sigvard and giggled. "At least we know not to do that. Glittery jodhpurs are not going to be welcome at any one's home."

Frowning, Lily replied, "You know it's all over our riding helmets, our jackets, as well as our faces, right? I just hope it will brush off or it doesn't glisten in daylight, or Mum's going to ask questions!"

Sasha looked at Lily and Chloe more carefully. "You're right about the helmets. I never noticed earlier. Let's try brushing it off when we get back. Nearly there."

Through the gate into the big horse paddock, Lily asked Sigvard to dim his magical glow.

"Of course," he replied, and the light shrunk around him like a lantern being turned down.

She wondered if her mother's horse Gracie would react to the unicorn, but thankfully she seemed unconcerned, and stayed grazing over by Kahurangi. Yawning as they crossed the paddock, she dismounted at the gate into the barnyard, the others doing the same. She was looking forward to bed. *Still don't know how we're going to get this unicorn dust off everything though.*

"Everyone keep super quiet now," she whispered. "Let's unsaddle here." She slipped off Rainbow and unsaddled him quickly, careful not to make any noise. "Chlo, will you hold the ponies while Sash and I take the saddles up to the barn? I'll bring back some brushes with the feed for Sigvard."

The sooner the unicorn was gone from being near the barn, the better. *Not that Mum or Dad are likely to see him, but we've still got to get back inside without being heard. Oh heck, what if Kuia is wandering around like she does sometimes in the middle of the night when she can't sleep?*

Crunch, crunch, crunch. Their footsteps on the gravel of the yards sounded enormously loud in the deep silence of the very early morning.

Lily's arms were loaded with two saddles, so Sasha unlatched the barn door.

C-r-e-a-k.

They froze, looking at each other in the dim moonlight.

"Well, the door's open now," Sasha whispered. "At least

it's not windy so we can leave it open as we put things away. What bucket can you give Sigvard with the feed that your mum won't notice is missing?"

Lily stepped carefully into the gloom of the barn. "I think there's an old one by the feed drums somewhere."

Fumbling, she managed to get the saddles put away.

"I'll take some brushes down and we'll give Rainbow a quick groom too." Sasha disappeared out the door.

Lily turned to the feed room. *There better not be any mice!* It couldn't be much darker as she took one careful step after another, hands stretched out in front. Bump. *That's the wall.* She felt along. *There's the door.* Along the feed room wall, hands and shuffling feet feeling for feed drums. Thud. She'd kicked one.

"That's the chaff bin," she whispered to herself, feeling beside it for the old bucket that should be there. "Ah, there it is."

Something scrabbled over her hand as she turned the bucket over to knock out any dust.

"Aarghh!" The heavy plastic bucket thudded to the floor. "Yuck, yuck, yuck!" Lily shook her hands, trying to get rid of that sensation of mouse feet running over her skin.

Suddenly she stopped, listening. Thankfully, all was silent. She'd been far too noisy. And the others were waiting!

Quickly, she felt for the bucket. Got it. Into the bins. Just the pony pellets. Three scoops. *Hopefully Mum won't notice.*

Along the wall, out the door into the main barn. The doorway was bright with starlight compared to the gloom of the barn, then she was off down the yard walking as quietly and quickly as she could on its gravel surface.

"There you are," Sasha hissed. "You've been ages."

"Sorry, a mouse jumped out of the bucket when I picked it up."

"Ooh, yuck!" Chloe whispered as she opened the gate for Lily.

"Here you are, Sigvard." Lily stopped in front of the big warrior unicorn who had his head down for Sasha to rub behind his ears. "I remembered this old bucket has a rope handle to replace its broken one, so I thought it might be easier for you to carry."

She put the bucket on the ground, holding the rope up so the unicorn could grab it in his mouth.

He lifted the bucket easily and rested it down again. "Perfect."

"Let the five weakest foals have a few mouthfuls each," Lily suggested, her voice low. "You don't want them to have too much in case they get an upset tummy. If there's any left, maybe some of the other foals could have a mouthful or two each. We'll bring some more tonight in our backpacks."

"Excellent. I must go. Thank you all. See you tonight." Snatching the bucket up, the unicorn trotted back across the paddock then jumped over the gate into the gloom of the forest.

"He's not shining his light," Sasha said as they slipped the bridles off their ponies with one last pat and turned them loose.

"Doesn't want to be seen, does he?" Lily latched the gate. "It was only us who needed the light to see, not the ponies or unicorns."

They walked back to the barn. Sasha asked, "Are we putting them at risk, asking him to light our way through the forest?"

"Well," Chloe whispered, "they are all grazing in the

open with their lights showing so they must feel quite safe on the farm."

"I guess so." Lily still felt worried.

They hung their bridles up and closed the barn carefully.

"And now to get back into the house without waking anyone," Lily murmured.

"I'm so tired, despite the dust stuff," Chloe said.

"I know." Sasha yawned.

"Let's try and wash off as much as we can in the laundry before we go inside," Chloe whispered.

"Good idea. There should be some paper towels so we can throw them away."

One by one, they crept up the back steps into the laundry room beside the back doors. Quietly, they dampened paper towels and wiped the glittery dust off as best they could in the near dark.

"Darn," Lily hissed. "We forgot to clean our helmets."

"I'll run down before breakfast and do it," Sasha replied.

Lily yawned. "Okay. Let's go to bed." They'd done everything they needed to with the unicorns tonight, so that was the main thing.

"And we'll do it all again tomorrow night," Sasha whispered as they undressed and slipped into bed.

Lily could hear the smile in Sasha's voice and smiled back even though she couldn't see. "I can't wait to see Ambrosius and the others again either."

"Me too," Chloe replied. "Good night."

Lily looked at her clock. "Good morning you mean. It's one o'clock."

There was no reply. She shut her eyes and slept.

———

The ponies clip-clopped tiredly down the Masterton's long drive.

"What a waste of time," Sasha grumbled for what seemed like the hundredth time.

The search for a hiding place had not gone well. Every park they'd visited during the hot, dusty morning around the streets of Whale Bay had something that made it impossible to consider trying to hide a hundred or so unicorns there. Too small, way too close to houses or shops, no grazing, no trees to hide amongst.

"It wasn't," Chloe repeated patiently. "Marking options off the list is still productive."

Feeling as frustrated as Sasha, Lily decided they had only one option. "We've got to check that big park over the highway."

"But how are we going to get there? You know we're not allowed to ride anywhere near the highway." Sasha's voice was grumpy. "And Chlo and I can't keep looking this afternoon."

"I know that. Maybe we can bike over there."

"But when? Mum said I could stay here again tonight, but I have to go with her to Susie's stupid dance thing all day tomorrow."

Chloe's disappointment was clear on her face. "I'd come if I could, Lil, you know that, right?"

Lily sighed. *And I need to train Rainbow, but one of us needs to keep trying to help the unicorns.* "It's okay. I'll bike over there. This afternoon if I can."

Chloe looked worried. "Are you sure, Lil? By yourself? Over the highway?"

"Haven't we agreed that it's possible the witch could get here by Sunday night? Ambrosius wants to move then, right? They've got to move somewhere, and what if this reserve is perfect and we didn't know until like Monday or something? It might be too late." Lily saw Chloe's face. "I'll be careful, honest. But one of us has got to do it, and I can, so I will."

Sasha didn't look any happier than Chloe. "If only I didn't have to go home, Lil, or I'd come with you."

"I know, Sash, it's okay. Really."

The driveway swung past the house where Lily's mother was sweeping the patio. She called out, "I'm leaving in ten minutes if the girls want a lift home."

Lily glanced from one friend to the other. They both nodded.

"Yes, please!" Lily called back, pressing her hot, sweaty pony into a trot. "Sorry, buddy, it's only a little further." She lowered her voice. "Just think of me biking all that way this afternoon."

"Oh, don't, Lily," Chloe implored. "I feel bad as it is."

They reached the tree-shaded cool of the horse yards with relief. "Just pop your guys in a yard and unsaddle." Lily slipped off Rainbow and let him into a pen. "I'll hose them down and put them out in the paddock."

Sasha had her chestnut gelding's halter on and saddle off in a flash, and headed for the barn with her gear. "Are you sure, Lil? I can run home along the road in a bit."

"Then you'll be late. Mum's driving right past anyway."

"Okay, thanks."

Chloe rubbed Angel's sweaty forehead, the palomino mare's gold hair sticking to her dark jodhpurs. "Thanks, Lily. I really appreciate it."

"I hope you'll come with us tonight, Chlo."

Chloe washed her hands under the hose Lily turned on to wash Rainbow. "I'll try to, if Mum will let me stay the night. I don't think I could sneak out of our house again. I was too frightened. I'll message you later when I've talked to Mum."

"Okay." Lily was worried about sneaking out again too. But they'd all managed it last night, so they'd just have to do it again. *And as many nights as the unicorns need us to help them.*

The toot of a car horn sent the girls scrambling out of the horse yards.

"Thanks, Lil, see you later," Sasha yelled as she raced after Chloe.

Running the hose over Rainbow's bright bay coat, Lily rinsed away the sweaty marks left by the saddle and girth. The pony stood, relaxed and head down. She wet a towel to wash his face, and he leaned into her hand as she got the itchy sweat off his forehead. "That's good, huh?" He snorted and nodded his head. She patted his soggy neck. "Tommy's turn now. Then Angel. Then I better find some lunch. I'm hungry."

Sweating, Lily slogged up the hill from town on her bike. Every push of the pedals was an effort as the afternoon got hotter and hotter.

"Thank goodness." She saw the entrance to the big park.

Free-wheeling through the gates, she saw very few cars in the car park, but along each side of the front section of the park were houses, lots of them.

The houses tick off the 'near humans' bit, hopefully.

There were many trees, some standing alone, others in clusters among wide swathes of grass and gullies full of native bush.

Plenty of hiding places and grazing too.

From the car park, the park got much wider, swooping up a big hill on one side and down into a valley on the other. There was a sign for a walking track to the Puketea stream.

That's water taken care of.

But, and she worried it was a big 'but', it was a long way from the unicorn's deserted farm, and mostly along the highway.

Still, it's the best option we've found so far, that's for sure.

Lily took a big drink from the bottle in her backpack as she looked around.

I've got good news for everyone, and thankfully it's downhill to town and flat most of the way home too.

Pleased she'd thought to say to her mum that she was cycling for her own fitness training – Mum was okay with that and it was partly true – Lily turned her bike and headed for home. *Now I just need to get safely through the crazy summer traffic in town.*

CHAPTER NINE

A message pinged on Lily's phone as she pushed her bike into the garage.

"*Does yr phone do video?*" Sasha asked. "*Can u set it up 2 video u jumping rainbow? In case u do something that causes him to buck.*"

"*Great idea!*" she replied. "*Will try 2day. Thx! Park is perfect. See u later.*"

"*Yay! Nice work!*" came Sasha's quick response.

The house was quiet as Lily opened the door. She would grab something to eat then get Rainbow. *Maybe everyone's gone down to the beach and left me some afternoon tea in the fridge.*

She froze, fridge door open.

Not the beach! They'll see the chasm!

Shoving the fridge door shut, Lily raced out the back door. She had no idea what she'd do if she found Mum, Liam and Kuia down on their private beach. But she had to check.

Did the unicorns fill the hole in enough? Did the high tide smooth out the sand?

Next thing there was a yelp and Lily thudded onto the path.

Sky scrabbled out from under her, licking her face, her arms, her legs, anywhere he could reach as she lay winded on the hot concrete.

"Geez, Sky, leave off." Lily pushed the apologetic dog away and rolled over onto her back, arm across her eyes against the sun.

Ow. That hurt.

"Illy! Illy!"

Ooufhh! Liam flopped onto her tummy in the toddler's version of a wrestling move.

"Ow, Liam, don't!" Lily pushed her little brother off onto the grass beside the path where he rolled around giggling.

The garden gate clanked shut.

"What are you two doing?" Mum leaned over Lily, blocking the sun.

"I tripped over Sky."

Mum chuckled. "And Liam took advantage of you being on the ground?"

"Yeah." Lily sat up, rubbing her stomach. She scowled at Liam, who was giggling harder than ever as Sky darted in to lick his face. "He did."

Getting to her feet, she brushed herself down. "Where have you been?" *Please don't say the beach!*

"Supermarket, then over to visit Mrs Tamariki." Mum headed inside, grocery bags in hand, the dog and toddler hard on her heels. "Kuia picked some herbs from her garden."

Relief flooded through Lily as she saw her grandmother pushing through the gate, her arms laden with greenery. She ran towards Kuia. "Can I help, Kuia?"

"There's more in the car, Lily, if you can bring it into the cool of the laundry."

"Okay."

"Careful of the bag of nettles."

"Gee, thanks."

Lily managed to get the nettles and other smelly green plant clippings inside for Kuia, who quickly put her to work stripping leaves from stems.

"Now run some clean water in the laundry tub and swish those deep green leaves around," Kuia instructed. With gloved hands, Kuia was picking the nettle leaves.

Once the leaves were washed, Lily had to spin them dry in Mum's salad spinner. "You better wash that well before I spin lettuce in it," Mum commented as Lily fetched it from the kitchen.

Some leaves were bundled up in a clean tea towel to rest in the fridge overnight and some went straight into a big pot, Kuia talking all the time about the different plants and how they could be used as a poultice or rub. It was quite interesting, but also confusing as there were lots of plants and lots of ways to use them.

Lily's thoughts drifted back to the unicorns. There wasn't much of the tonic left.

"Kuia, I meant to ask you earlier. Do you think we could make some more of the tonic I gave my friend with the burnt pony please?" She hated lying, but what was the alternative? She swallowed against the sick feeling in her tummy. "She dropped the bottle and it smashed."

Out of the corner of her eye, she saw Kuia's brown gaze study her for a moment, and she tried not to squirm, focusing on swishing the leaves in a clean batch of water before she spun them dry.

"She wouldn't want to give her pony too much at a time, you know. That would be very dangerous."

Lily glanced up, but Kuia was now looking at the big pot she was stirring on a gas burner on the laundry bench.

"I'm sure she didn't do that. She said she tripped over taking it back into their stable."

"Okay then, as long as she doesn't think a double or triple dose will make him heal faster. I can make some more from the herbal tinctures I have with me."

"Thank you. She will really appreciate it."

Kuia nodded as she stirred. "How did you get the herbs to her anyway? No one's been to pick anything up since I made it yesterday."

What's with the questions, Kuia? Lily wanted to ask. *What does it matter to you anyway?* She felt queasy having to tell another lie. "We visited when we went riding this morning and dropped it off."

"Okay." Kuia put down the big spoon. "Come and watch me measure the tinctures. I'll show you how to combine them safely."

Lily stood beside Kuia, watching carefully. *Thank goodness she agreed to make more tonic. I had no idea what I was going to say if she said no.*

Finally, she'd tidied up the laundry to Mum's expectation. "I don't want nettle stings all through the washing."

Eating a banana with one hand and holding a bunch of carrots to share among the horses in the other, Lily managed to get out of the house with just enough sunlight left to have half an hour in the arena. The fresh bottle of burn-healing tonic was at the back door, ready to take tonight – or, as Kuia thought, deliver to her *friend* tomorrow. Her phone was fully charged, and she thought she could prop it in the cup of a jump stand, so it pointed in the right direction to video her and Rainbow jumping.

"I don't know why I haven't thought of this before, Rainbow," Lily said as she brushed her pony and tacked him up. "We won't take long, considering we have another ride to see you know who tonight, but the video is a good idea from Sasha."

They rode into the arena. "I don't really want to get bucked off again, so maybe Kuia's tonic has already helped, and you'll jump properly now." Rainbow snorted as she asked him to trot and they circled to warm up. "But if not, maybe the video will give me a clue what's happening with the doubles if you still buck."

She stopped Rainbow beside the jump stand and set the phone to record. "Okay, let's try this."

Pushing her heels down in the stirrups, she pressed Rainbow into a canter and circled him round a couple of times. Nerves swirled making her feel sick again. Don't think about falling off, she told herself firmly. *Just look ahead over the second jump like Mum tells you to do.*

They headed for the combination of two jumps. Over the first, one stride and over the second, and...bang! Rainbow pig-jumped the instant he landed. Lily shot out of the saddle but managed to pull herself straight again. They cantered fast around the arena, Rainbow tugging at the reins and Lily's shaking hands only just managing to hold the upset pony.

Okay, she told herself, breathing hard, *I expected that. Now I've got to turn around and jump from the other direction so there's a video from both sides.*

"Steady, pony, steady." She turned Rainbow in a tight circle to slow him to a walk. He let out a deep breath with a shudder that shook her in the saddle. Maybe she was just upsetting him. Should she go and talk to her mum?

But I want to solve this myself!

Letting the reins loose, she encouraged her pony to stretch his neck and relax. Lily lay forward over Rainbow's withers, her head close to his. "We can figure this out, can't we?" His ears flicked back and forward as he listened. "Okay." Lily made a decision. "I'll talk with Mum if I can't see anything obvious from the video, so let's jump back in the other direction so that's on video too."

She closed her eyes for a moment, visualising going over the two jumps cleanly, then they circled to approach the double from the other side. She leaned forward, the reins slipping through her fingers perfectly to let Rainbow stretch his head as he cleared the jump. One canter stride, then up and over again.

Uh-oh! Rainbow arched into a buck, all four feet drawn together as he sprang up, sending Lily flying forward over his shoulder.

Whump!

Ow...

Just like the other day, Rainbow stopped as soon as he got rid of Lily. He nuzzled her back as Lily lay face down in the sandy arena. She pushed up onto her knees to brush the sand off. "Oh, pony, what are we going to do?"

Rainbow stood there, as placid as anything. With a sigh, Lily got to her feet. "Let's have a look at the video."

She walked back to the jump stand to pick up the phone, Rainbow coming of his own accord behind her. Watching intently as she jumped in the left-hand direction, Lily saw her lower leg swing back along and up Rainbow's side on the second jump. "Wow, I never knew I did that."

She fast-forwarded to the jumps in the other direction.

"Oh, I do that with both legs! Perhaps that's it." Her legs rubbed right up Rainbow's sensitive flank, a ticklish place on horse and where rodeo folk tie the flank strap to make horses and bulls buck.

Excited she might have solved the problem, Lily said, "Shall we try again, Rainbow?" She set the phone to video again. "Do I do it with singles or just doubles? I wonder why no one's ever said anything about it before." She swung up into the saddle, feeling better about jumping her pony than she had for weeks.

A quick canter to warm up and Lily faced her pony to the jumps. "Remember," she said out loud, "heels down the whole time."

They went over the first jump. Perfect. Second jump, legs in absolutely the right position. He cleared it!

"We did it!"

She took Rainbow around the whole course of seven jumps, repeating in her mind heels down, heels down. He cleared every jump – including the double – perfectly.

"You beauty!" Lily clapped her hand on Rainbow's neck. "I'm sorry I was mucking things up for you, buddy. Here was me wondering what you were doing wrong, when it was me."

She slipped from the saddle, patting the bay gelding and rubbing that spot on his forehead that every horse loves.

Relief flooded through her. "I can't believe it. We're ready to go to the Pony Club champs qualifier now." She lowered her voice. "We just need to find the unicorns some-where safe to hang out for a few weeks while Brökk gets better and everything's sweet."

Sasha and Chloe were at Lily's house when she came in, on

the lawn playing with Liam while Lily's father cooked sausages on the barbecue.

"Hey, you're here, Chlo. That's great!" Lily plopped down on the lawn. "I solved the problem with doubles!"

"Really?" Sasha grinned. "That's brilliant. What was wrong?"

"The video idea was the bit that was brilliant, Sash. I'll show you." Lily played the clip.

"Oh, look at your legs!" Sasha exclaimed.

"I know, right?" Lily replied.

"I've never noticed that before. We're probably all busy watching Rainbow rather than you." Chloe leaned in to restart the video. "Ouch. Are you okay from that fall?"

"I'm fine. But isn't it weird that not even Mum has ever said about it?"

Lily's mother came out onto the patio, carrying a salad. "What haven't I said anything about?"

"Look, Mum." Lily jumped up with her phone to show her mother.

"No, I hadn't noticed either, which isn't very good, is it, but you do tend to practice jumping by yourselves."

"And Mum, I did the jumps again, making sure I kept my legs down, and Rainbow jumped beautifully!"

Tessa gave Lily a hug. "That's very good problem solving, Lily. Well done!"

Lily danced away across the sunny lawn with its view out to the sea. "I'm so happy! Now I can train properly for the Pony Club championships qualifier." She turned back to her friends. "It's all on now, you know! We'll all be battling for the under thirteen-year-old team positions."

Sasha jumped up, her fists raised in a boxing stance. "Bring it on!"

Lily laughed, gently slapping her friend's hands down, as she skipped by.

"You know it's over to Mr Conrad, the selector," Chloe chipped in.

"Yeah," Sasha said with a sigh. "And he's never liked me, so it will be you and Lily for the team to go to Hawke's Bay for the championship."

"Well, if I get selected, then I have to convince my mother to let me go," said Chloe.

Lily stopped dancing then. *How awful not to have your mother support you in the thing you loved most.* She dashed to hug Chloe. "We'll help you convince her, because we'll all be going anyway to support each other, no matter who gets selected."

Chloe smiled her gentle smile. "Thanks, Lil, you're the best."

"Hey, I'll help too." Sasha threw her arms around them both. "Whether two of us, only one or even none of us get selected, we're always gonna support each other, right?"

"Of course!" Lily giggled. *It felt so good to have solved her problem of jumping the doubles, surely everything else would work out too.*

"The woes of the world, you girls have, don't you?" Lily's father piled up the cooked sausages and lamb chops. "You'll feel better after some dinner."

"Go and help Kuia with knives and forks, all of you," Tessa instructed as she carried plates to the outside table. "And grab a jersey! It might be December, but it's still cool outside."

Pushing each other and laughing, the three popped through the sliding door and nearly knocked Kuia over.

"Sorry, Kuia, let me take that." Lily took the cutlery from her grandmother. "Is there anything else?"

"Garlic bread in the oven. Put it on a board. And the tomato sauce."

"Got it!" Sasha ran for the kitchen.

"I'll get the jerseys." Chloe headed for the bedroom.

Lily went out with Kuia, her mind turning to tonight's ride to see the unicorns and tell them about the park she visited this afternoon. *I can't wait to tell Ambrosius the good news.*

CHAPTER TEN

The moon was even brighter as the ponies walked across the big horse paddock to the forest gate.

Chloe spoke quietly. "Good idea to hide our tack under the paddock trees when we went down to say goodnight to the ponies."

Lily smiled. "I have good ideas sometimes."

"Much easier than worrying about the barn door waking your parents up," said Sasha. "I didn't think they were ever going to go to bed. Let's trot now. Sigvard will be waiting."

"He said he'd be there an hour after moonrise, so we're okay," Lily replied as she let Rainbow trot after the others.

She was just as keen as her friends to see the unicorns again. The tonic and her tablet bumped around in her backpack, and she couldn't wait to see whether Brökk was stronger. Sasha and Chloe had horse feed from their own supplies in their backpacks for the mage and the foals. And Chloe had a great idea about how to keep the unicorns off the highway for a lot of the journey to the big park.

They reached the gate.

"He's not there!" Sasha slipped off Tommy to undo the latch and push the heavy gate open. "Where is he?" She looked up at Lily, worried.

"He'll probably be here soon." Lily nudged Rainbow through the gate after Angel.

"Let's keep going." Sasha closed the gate before swinging up into the saddle. "There might be something wrong, and it's not that dark among the trees with the moon."

"No, Sasha! Let's wait for Sigvard," Chloe said. "It *is* too dark, and we don't have the torch. What if the ponies get hurt?"

Sasha didn't answer, but kept Tommy standing with the other ponies where the deep gloom of the tall pines started.

The thud of fast-moving hoof beats sounded through the trees.

A silver unicorn appeared.

"It's Ambrosius!" Lily rode forward to meet the unicorn king.

"What's wrong? Where's Sigvard?" Sasha asked anxiously.

"He's busy, so I came to accompany you myself," replied Ambrosius as the glow of light flared around him. "Are you ready? Let us go." His voice was impatient, anxious, and immediately he leapt into a swift canter. Lily had to push Rainbow to keep up.

She rode beside Ambrosius for a few minutes, her pony practically galloping on the rough forestry track, before he seemed to realise he was going too fast for the ponies and slowed a fraction.

She could feel great tension radiating from the unicorn.

Something bad must have happened. "What's wrong, Ambrosius?"

"We need to get back to the herd quickly. Mikaela and Guilio can sense Abellona."

Lily gasped. "No!"

Sasha and Chloe, riding abreast behind, echoed her horror.

"They are scouting to see if Abellona has actually reached this land. Sigvard's warriors guard the herd while he accompanies Mikaela."

"But what will you do if she's here? Will you move tonight? Can Brökk move? What about the smallest foals?" The questions tumbled out of Lily's mouth as soon as they formed. It was hard to think coherently while racing through the forest late at night and filled with worry for the unicorns.

"I am undecided. Brökk is not yet at full strength, but much improved. The foals are also stronger. If we could determine how far away Abellona actually is, that would help me decide. But I feel one more night of rest and your tonic – did you bring more?"

"Yes."

"Good. Another night here would make a great difference to them all, but especially Brökk. The stress of moving the whole herd and him feeling like he needs to be able to protect us could set back his recovery."

"The big park we looked at on the map, Ambrosius, it's perfect," Lily said over the thud of four sets of hooves. "Chloe has worked out a way to reach it which uses the main road for just a short way."

"That sounds promising, thank you. We will look at a map on your tablet, yes?"

"I brought it with me."

"Good. Now, let us press on as fast as we can."

Lily urged her willing pony on, the others pressed close behind. The long strides of the unicorn thundered beside her, a counter-beat to the thud of her heart.

Oh, how she hoped everyone was okay and that Abellona really wasn't that close. *One more day would make such a difference for the unicorns. But maybe they should move tonight, to be safe.*

They quickly reached the gate out onto Sanderson Road. The unicorn soared over it without hesitation as Lily flung herself off Rainbow to deal with the latch. She could see the worry on her friends' faces as they went through the gate, but no one said anything as they cantered up the road verge and swept into the farm gateway. The glow around Ambrosius flicked out. Chloe gasped, but the ponies didn't hesitate as they followed the unicorn in the moonlight.

The ponies will certainly be getting fitter with all this fast work. The random thought crossed Lily's mind as they slowed near the herd. Ambrosius led them through clusters of unicorns gathered near the tree-lined edges of the big paddock they'd made their home for the past few days.

Not one unicorn had their light showing, although a brief glimmer would pop up around a foal from time to time. A hushed whicker of warning from the foal's mother, and the light would disappear. Most were grazing in quick snatches, lifting their heads to look around and keep an eye on their leader.

The girls were quiet as their ponies caught their breath, standing beside Ambrosius who had his head high, scanning the sky.

He's looking for Guilio. Lily couldn't see the milky-white pegasus anywhere among the unicorns. Sigvard or

Mikaela weren't visible either – both Sasha and Chloe were looking around anxiously for their favourites.

Lily caught the salty scent of the sea in the breeze blowing in from the coast, mingling with the distinctive pine aroma of the forest between them and the beach. Her tummy was tight with nerves, waiting for something, anything that gave them an idea where the dangerous Abellona was.

A whoosh of giant wings broke the silence and Guilio swept into land beside his leader.

"Sire, I have left Mikaela and Sigvard at the beach where we arrived. She can sense Abellona more strongly by the hour but is still finding it difficult to judge how far away she actually is. Mikaela's best estimate remains twelve to twenty-four hours."

"Thank you," Ambrosius replied. "Not much has changed since the last report. Twelve hours means we should move tonight. Twenty-hour hours means we can let Brökk rest another day."

"Yes, Sire, like Mikaela, I wish we had something more definite to tell you."

"Of course, Guilio. I know Mikaela is doing her best," the unicorn king said with a nod. "She is young in years and experience as a sensory and will take some time to refine her skills to Viveka's level. We all sorely miss Viveka."

"As do I," the pegasus replied.

"Who's Viveka?" Sasha whispered to Lily.

"Don't know," she whispered back. "Have to ask Ambrosius later."

The unicorn king continued, "I must admit I'd hoped for something that gave me a clearer sense of whether we should attempt to move tonight or not."

He looked at the herd gathered around him, all seeking

any scrap of information from their king. "Where is Brökk? I seek his counsel." He glanced at the girls. "And he should have more of Lily's tonic just as soon as he can."

"I'll get some water, Ambrosius. Sasha and Chloe can start offering the pony nuts to the foals."

"You start with the foals as well, Lily. Give them their tonic while I find Brökk." Ambrosius trotted into the trees. "Guilio, please return to Sigvard and Mikaela and report back if there is any change."

"Of course, Sire." The pegasus's wings opened with a sudden crack as he leapt into the air. A few swift wing strokes and he was flying low across the pine forest back to the beach and the others.

Lily was pleased to have something to do. She let Rainbow go, so he could graze, the stirrups run up the leathers and his reins safely knotted around his neck. But he followed her over to the trough where she found the collapsible bucket empty of the tonic she'd left for Brökk that morning.

"Sash, here's the bucket Sigvard bought over with the feed," she called quietly, feeling awkward disturbing the uneasy silence around the herd tonight. It was such a contrast to last night when foals raced each other back and forward, neighing to each other with the simple joy of running freely, and mares whinnying to call their racing babies to return. Tonight everyone was anxious.

With a fresh batch of tonic diluted in water, she looked around for Eva and her foal Lief. "There they are," she said to Rainbow, who stayed with her as she walked over. Sasha and Chloe carried the rope-handled bucket, now full of pony nuts, between them.

She offered Lief the tonic, and the dark grey foal drank eagerly. "I wonder where Brökk and Ambrosius are."

"Everything feels weird, doesn't it?" Chloe looked around.

"Very weird. Like waiting for the dentist, but worse." Lily gently pushed the colt away from the tonic. "That's enough for you, Lief. Have some grain from the other bucket."

She ran her hand down Eva's neck. To be able to touch a unicorn, any unicorn, was still an amazing feeling. "Do you know where the smallest filly and her mother are, Eva?"

"In the group next to that big tree," replied the mare in her silvery voice.

"Thank you. Do you feel Lief is stronger now?"

"Oh, yes, he's nearly fully recovered from the long journey here, aren't you, son?"

The colt nodded his baby head as he crunched another mouthful of horse feed.

"I think your tonic has been a big help," said Eva. "All the mares are saying they've never seen their foals return to normal as quickly after such a long trek before."

Lily smiled. "That's really good news, thank you."

She went over to the next group with the little filly and her mother while Lief finished his share of the feed with Chloe and Sasha.

"Hello, sweetie." The foal stepped forward shyly to drank as her mother stood close. Lily tried to see if the foal had any other injuries she could treat with the balm, but each time she lifted a hand to run it down the filly's leg, the unicorn mare moved her ivory spike in Lily's direction. She tried all her best soothing sounds and murmurings, but the mare wasn't having any of it.

If only Ambrosius could assure her I won't hurt the foal. Where is he? I feel even more nervous without him around, and I can't be sure which other three foals need more tonic.

Chloe and Sasha carried the feed bucket over for the little filly.

"Put the bucket down and step back," Lily suggested. "Her mama is very nervous."

A loud neigh cut through the anxious atmosphere around the herd.

"Lily!" Ambrosius's voice called from the trees. "Bring the tonic."

"It's Ambrosius! Quick."

Lily ran as fast as she could carrying the half-full bucket. She shouted, "Don't let her eat too much and get a sore stomach."

Stumbling down a tree-lined bank, Lily found Ambrosius locking horns with Brökk. "What's happened?"

"Brökk is trying to cast a cloaking spell across the herd." Ambrosius puffed with the effort of pushing Brökk's horn away. "But he's not strong enough to hold it for more than a few minutes."

The smaller, but still powerful unicorn mage snorted and stepped back, his eyes angry as they flicked from Ambrosius to Lily.

"No magic, Brökk!" Ambrosius instructed. "Save your energy. We need you as close to full strength as possible for when we move the herd."

Anxiously, Lily watched the unicorns. What would Brökk do?

"The other thing, Brökk," Ambrosius said, his eyes firmly on the mage, "which you surely know better than anyone, is that any pulse of magic will lead Abellona to the herd."

Sometimes it seemed to Lily that Ambrosius and Brökk were kind of equals – Ambrosius was obviously the herd's leader, but Brökk could wield powerful magic, even if he wasn't at full strength. Biting her lip, she waited for Brökk to respond. Would he use his magic against Ambrosius?

After several tense moments, Brökk lowered his head with a heartfelt sigh. "Sire, I apologise. I thought I was strong enough now." He sucked in a breath then let it out with another sad sigh. "I was responsible for bringing us here and not being able to move to a safer place. I want to do what I can to protect the herd."

Ambrosius lowered his head beside Brökk's. "My friend, you bought us away from Abellona and what you know was certain capture. We could not have achieved that without you. But we can't risk drawing Abellona directly to us until you regain your strength."

"I can only apologise, Ambrosius. I don't know what I was thinking. I do not like being able to contribute in my usual way."

"I understand but am frustrated that you may have put us in more danger with your actions." His voice was grim, and Brökk's head dropped again. "Let us hope Mikaela can get a better sense of Abellona soon. I came to ask if you could help Mikaela with that. As long as it does not tax your strength."

Brökk nodded. "It's not really my speciality, Sire, but I'll try."

"Good. Mikaela will appreciate any support we can offer. In the meantime, let Sigvard and I look after the herd as you continue to recover. Everyone is doing their best to help me determine when we should move."

"As you say, Ambrosius." Brökk lifted his head.

Ambrosius looked around at Lily. "Will you bring the tonic please, Lily?" He saw Sasha and Chloe waiting at the top of the bank. "We'll come up to you girls in a minute."

Lily stepped towards the mage and set down the bucket.

"Thank you, Lily," Brökk said, as he went to drink.

Lily smiled, relieved that Brökk ended up agreeing with Ambrosius. "You really need to thank my grandmother, but she'd be surprised to hear you speak to her."

Ambrosius lightened the mood with a chuckle. "I'm sure she would be. When you are finished, Brökk, let us get back to the herd. The girls have foals to tend to, and I want you to put your mind – but not your magic – to sensing any magic around us."

The unicorns trotted up the slope, and Lily clambered up behind them, heading for the trough to make a new batch of tonic. By the time she was ready, Ambrosius had the other small foals and their mothers gathered around Chloe and Sasha, so it was a quick matter to ensure each foal received their share of tonic and food.

"Brökk, have you eaten? Would you like more tonic?" Lily asked.

The mage and his leader stood looking out over the forest to the coastline a few kilometres away. The moonlight highlighted the dark intensity of Brökk's eyes as he swung to look at Lily. "Please." He dipped his head to drink. "And another bucket after this."

"Are you sure? Kuia said not to have too much at one time."

"Leave it with me to drink later as you did last night."

"Okay. Hey, girls, do you want to put balm on Brökk's burns?"

"Sure." Sasha took the balm from Lily, who headed for the trough to mix more tonic. "What can you sense, Brökk? How does it work?"

"All unicorns can sense magic to a certain degree, but sensories like Mikaela have a special gift. They are much more highly attuned to the subtle resonance emanating from the creature generating the magic."

Chloe soothed balm on the burn on his chest. "Can you feel anything, Brökk?"

"There is a faint magical vibration in the atmosphere, but that may have been from my failed cloaking spell." His voice was solemn.

Lily set the tonic down and patted him. She didn't like seeing him upset but couldn't understand why he'd tried to cast a spell if he wasn't strong enough. Maybe his anxiety to get back to full strength affected his ability to think clearly.

The girls stood with the unicorns, looking over the forest and bush towards the sea. All was quiet, just the sporadic sounds of unicorns snatching grass around them and a native owl making its distinctive 'more-pork' call.

"Is the beach a better place for Mikaela?" Lily asked Ambrosius.

"The chasm is the first place she'll sense Abellona's magic, and what she can sense is definitely stronger there."

Lily nodded. That seemed logical. "Is the chasm still visible? I've been worried that my family would see it if they go down to the beach."

"It's a sunken patch near the high tide line now, so not too obvious," he replied.

"I've been wanting to go and close it properly," added Brökk.

"And you know why I said it's just fine as it is." Ambrosius looked at the mage with a stern gaze. "We're thankful Lily's family hasn't been to the beach since we arrived."

"How do you know that?" Lily asked, surprised.

"We have sentries posted, of course."

"Oh! We've never seen them."

The unicorn king snorted. "They wouldn't be very good unicorn sentries if you had. Now let us look at your tablet so Chloe can show us the route we will take tomorrow."

Lily pulled the tablet out and gave it to Chloe, who held it so the unicorns could look over her shoulders at the screen.

"We're here on Sanderson Road. We want to get *here*, to the big park behind town. The fastest route is along the highway. But if we turn right out of Sanderson Road and go along the highway in the other direction for a short way, we can turn up into this forestry block and use the dirt road. It takes us quite close to park. We'd just need to weave through a few suburban streets to get to it."

"That looks excellent, Chloe, thank you. A much better route," Ambrosius said. "Less time on the main road. Less visible from the air through the forest. And now I think you girls should head home to sleep."

"Oh, Ambrosius..." Lily looked at him. "It's so nice spending time with you all, even if I am worried about Abellona."

"And we want to see Sigvard and Mikaela," Sasha added.

"They may not be back for some time. Anyway, I have made up my mind. If Brökk cannot sense any strong magic and Guilio has not come with any urgent messages from Mikaela, then we are not moving tonight. We will all rest and continue to regain our strength." He looked at the girls. "And therefore, the best thing you can do to help us tonight is go home, get a good sleep, and Sigvard or I will meet you at the gate an hour before moonrise tomorrow night."

Lily glanced at Sasha who nodded and said, "Well, I guess we're going home then."

Chloe yawned. "I'm tired, even if you aren't."

"I could sprinkle some more of my special dust if you like, so you get home safely," Ambrosius offered.

"No, thanks." Lily stepped back from the unicorn with a grin. "Mum went mad when she saw my pillowcase this morning while changing my bed."

His deep chuckle rolled around them as Sasha laughed. "Then you blamed the glitter bomb on my little sister."

"First thing I could think of!" Lily turned to look for Rainbow.

"Not sure your mum believed it."

"Ha-ha, no."

"Imagine if it had been *my* mum," Chloe said as they walked over to their ponies grazing together. "I'd have been grounded for a week, no matter what I said."

Lily groaned. "Oh, yeah, that would not have been good."

Within a few minutes, they caught the ponies, tightened girths and mounted.

Lily looked around the herd. The mares had gone back to grazing, their foals alongside. The tension they felt earlier seemed to have eased, although the herd was still in darkness except for the odd pop of light appearing around a foal then disappearing again.

They rode over to Ambrosius and Brökk who were still watching out to the coast.

"Good, you are ready," Ambrosius said. "Let us get going. Brökk, you will graze and rest like the others."

"Of course, Sire." The mage nodded.

"Fredek! Isak!" He called two unicorns standing sentry near the forest edge over. "You're in charge of the herd's safety while I'm gone. Send for me urgently if anything changes."

"Yes, Sire," the tall silver-grey unicorns replied in unison.

"I've left more tonic for you, Brökk." Lily pointed to the bucket by the trough. "And grain."

"Thank you." Brökk turned to the trough as Ambrosius led the way across the paddock to the driveway and home.

CHAPTER ELEVEN

"Beach! Beach! Beach!" Liam shouted as he thudded down the hall.

"Oh, no!" Lily fell out of bed, her legs tangled in the sheet, and landed on top of Sasha on the camp bed.

"Ouch!"

"Sorry! Get up! We have to stop them." Lily hissed. "The unicorns need to keep watch at our beach. They can't have humans in the way." She ran out of her bedroom door, leaving Sasha and Chloe to scramble after her.

"Morning, love." Dad strode into the hall to scoop Liam into his arms, the toddler screaming with delight.

"Uh, hi, Dad. Are you going to the beach?"

"Ask your mum. She was talking about it." He headed into Liam's room. "You girls better go and get breakfast while I dress this monster."

"Not monster!" Liam protested.

"You're a ticklish monster!" Dad laughed as he tickled Liam. The toddler's giggles echoed along the hall as Dad took him into his bedroom.

"Come on." Lily saw the girls were up. She dressed

quickly, and they ran into the kitchen filled with the Sunday morning smell of bacon.

Lily's tummy rumbled as she wrapped Kuia in a hug. "Morning, Kuia."

"Hello, my darling." Kuia smiled her wrinkly smile. "And how are you this morning? And your friends?"

"Good, thanks." *Tired, actually, but you'll ask why if I say that. And I'm worried for the unicorns and scared about tonight too. But I guess I'm not lying because I am happy that we found the unicorns somewhere safe to go and they're going there tonight...*

"How many eggs, Lily?" Mum asked from the stove. "What about you, Sasha? Chloe?"

"One, please, Mum." She sat down beside Kuia who poured her a mug of milky tea.

"Same, thanks, Mrs Masterton," Chloe replied.

"Two for me, please," Sasha added as she joined Chloe opposite Lily. "Beach! Ask!" she mouthed at Lily, who waved her hand in a 'slow down' kind of way.

Lily passed bowls from the pile at the end of the table. "Do you want cereal and yogurt?"

The girls started eating as Liam ran in, wearing just his swimming togs, Dad close behind.

Sasha's eyes went wide in alarm. "It's a bit cold for togs, isn't it?" her voice squeaked.

Lily swallowed a mouthful. "Are you going to the beach, Mum?"

"Liam wants to, as you can see." Mum put a plate piled with toast on the table. "I've tried to explain we need to wait until late morning for the best tide, but you know what he's like."

Lily tried to smile as Dad caught Liam and put him in the highchair, but a sick feeling grew in her stomach. They needed to keep her family away from their private beach, but how?

Then, an idea.

"How about we go to Whale Bay beach for a change, Mum? It has that lovely shallow bit that's great for Liam. I could look after him if you want to go for a long swim." Lily's mother used to compete in triathlons and still liked to swim, bike and run to keep fit.

Sasha grinned at Lily and gave her a quick thumbs up.

"Maybe." Mum set down a big dish of bacon and eggs. "What do you think, John? Are you coming?"

Dad sat down. "Not if Kuia's happy to mind the kids."

"I'm not a baby, Dad!" Lily interjected. "I said I'd look after Liam."

"And the law says you need an adult supervising around water."

Kuia chuckled. "You're in charge of Liam, Lily, don't worry. I can't run that fast."

"Thanks Ma. So yes, Lily, we can go down to the main beach for an hour or so later this morning."

Yes! Lily did a mental fist pump. She spooned up the last of her cereal, keeping her face down, not wanting them to see her relief. "Cool. It will make a nice change."

"Always seems a bit odd you offering to look after Liam." Mum handed out plates with the requested number of eggs to the girls. "But I'm not going to give up the chance for a swim."

Lily could feel the girls both watching her as she took the plate from her mother. "Thank you. I do look after him sometimes, you know."

Mum smiled. "Usually when you want something. What do you want this time?"

"Nothing!" *Help, this is getting more complicated than it needs to be.*

"If you say so, but we'll see. Are you girls coming too?"

"Ah, no..." Chloe stumbled her reply as she often did with Lily's forthright mother. "Not today, Mrs Masterton. I've got to go to church with my mother this morning."

"I've told you to call me Tessa, Chloe. What about you, Sasha? You're a beach girl from way back."

"I'd love to, but Mum insists I go to Susie's dance competition today." Sasha sighed as she flipped her phone open to check the time. "And I better eat quickly, get Tommy and head home soon or she'll kill me." She put her phone down and concentrated on clearing her plate.

Kuia chuckled again. "What dramatic words. In my day, you were only worried you were going to get a hiding."

"Ma!" Mum frowned. "That kind of punishment would be regarded as child abuse nowadays. Well, you girls better get moving if you're finished." She started collecting plates.

"I'll help!" Sasha jumped up.

Chloe nudged Lily as they stood up with their plates. "What about Angel?" she whispered. "Can she stay here?"

Lily whispered back. "Ask Dad. It will be fine."

"Um, Mr Masterton?"

Dad looked up from wiping egg and crumbs from Liam's face. "Yes, Chloe."

"Is it okay, um, if Angel stays another day, please?" She glanced at Lily, who nodded encouragement. "I need to talk with someone at Pony Club about the horse that's bullying her and won't be able to do that until tomorrow."

Lily crossed her fingers behind her back. All this lying made her uncomfortable.

"No problem." He got Liam out of his highchair. "Don't know why you don't graze Angel here. There's plenty of room, and you're always over here riding with Lily anyway."

"Thank you. I'll talk with Mum about it again. But you know how she likes me to do things the way she thinks is proper."

Dad laughed. "So, it seems."

The girls made quick work of stacking the dishwasher and wiping the table, before grabbing their gear from Lily's room and heading for the barn.

"I'm so worried about tonight, I don't know how I'm going to concentrate with my tutor later." Chloe opened the horse paddock gate.

Lily sighed as they walked to the horses standing under their favourite trees. "I know. It's going to be a l-o-n-g day, waiting and hoping Brökk's well enough."

"And that Abellona hasn't turned up in the meantime and captured the whole herd." Sasha held out the bread crusts Lily's mum gave them. "Here, one for each. Gracie too."

Lily stared at Sasha, horrified. "That could happen, couldn't it? And we'd never know."

Sasha nodded. "Sounds like she could appear any time, doesn't it? Would she care about possibly being seen in daylight? She'd just hunt the herd down as fast as she could."

"Aren't you worried for the unicorns, Sasha? Kind of sounds like you're expecting that to happen." Chloe said, her voice trembling as they reached the ponies.

"Of course, I'm worried. It's hours since we've seen them and I'm terrified, especially for Sigvard and Mikaela who are closest to where Abellona will probably arrive." Sasha sniffed as she slipped the halter on Tommy. "But what can I do today? I've got to go to this stupid dance thing when I'd rather saddle up and ride over to the unicorns right now and make sure they're okay."

That sick feeling in Lily's tummy came back, and she could see tears welling in Chloe's eyes.

What could they do?

Well, the others couldn't do anything – they had to get home – so what could *she* do?

"It's only eight o'clock. I'll bring Rainbow up to the barn with you." She took hold of Rainbow's forelock and urged him to walk with the other ponies. "I'll tell Mum I'm going to do some training in the cross-country paddock for a while before we go to the beach. There's a gate at the top which goes straight into the forest. You can't see it from the house like the other gate."

"It's eight o'clock? I've got to hurry." Chloe started jogging. Angel trotted beside her even though Chloe hadn't haltered her.

"What are you going to do, Lil?" Tommy tagged at Sasha so he could follow Angel. "Hang on, pony."

Lily clicked to get Rainbow trotting too. "Go see the herd, obviously. I've got a couple of hours easily."

Chloe hustled everyone through the gate, leaving an anxious Angel behind. "You're staying here, girl. Go find Gracie." She patted her palomino mare and ran after the others to the barn. "And you'll text us? Let us know the herd's okay?"

"Of course."

"Thanks!" Chloe swung her backpack on. "I better get walking. Thanks for keeping Angel here, Lil. I'll see you tonight. Hope I can get out okay. That's almost scaring me more than the thought of Abellona."

Shutting Rainbow into a yard by the barn, Lily hugged Chloe. "You'll be fine. Give yourself plenty of time and clear the way before you go to bed. Remember the dog toy here?" Chloe smiled and nodded.

Sasha wrapped them both in a bear hug. "You won't trip over anything – there's never anything out of place at your house! You'll be right, mate. See you later."

Chloe waved as she set off down the drive towards home, church and extra tutoring.

Going into the barn to get her gear, Sasha said, "Wish I could come with you."

Lily grabbed Rainbow's tack and the box of brushes. "I know. But you have to go support your sister. Is your dad going too?"

They groomed the ponies quickly. "I hope so. I haven't seen much of him lately." She picked out Tommy's feet, Lily matching her actions with Rainbow. "Mind you, Mum will just go on and on at him all day, so it's probably nicer for him if he's not there."

Lily flipped the saddle cloth over Rainbow's shiny bay back. "I wish there was something I could do to help, Sash."

"There isn't, but thanks." Sasha tightened the girth. "Well, Tommy, it's time to leave the peace and harmony of Lily's home."

"Come here, you." Lily wrapped Sasha in a tight hug. "Hopefully there's no fighting today anyway. I'll text you when I know more."

"You better!" Sasha swiped a tear off her cheek and turned to mount her chestnut.

"Bye!" Lily closed the gate onto the driveway behind Sasha. "I'll just run and tell Mum we're having a quick ride," she said to her pony. "Then we'll go."

Lily dismounted to get Rainbow through the gate from the

horse paddock into the cross-country paddock. Kahurangi tried to push through to Gracie and Angel.

"Move back, girl." She opened the gate just wide enough for Rainbow. "I haven't got time to catch you again if you get out." She swung the gate shut millimetres behind Rainbow's rump, into the faces of Gracie and Angel who wanted to follow. "You guys!"

Lily swung up onto Rainbow and walked him along the fence-line, all the mares following on their respective side of the fence. They swung left up the far edge of this paddock where it backed into the pine forest. The hill rose before them and Lily leaned forward to help Rainbow as he bounded upward. Kahurangi ran with them for a while then turned back to the others.

"Good fitness work, buddy." Lily pulled Rainbow up at the top, the pony breathing hard in the cool morning breeze blowing in off the sea. She could see right over their farm to the bush and the beach. "I forgot how great it is up here. You can see right along Whale Bay beach and back towards town. There's Sasha's place along the road too."

She turned to the back boundary of the paddock. "Let's hope it's not padlocked."

They trotted over.

"Curses, it is."

She looked around. Along a bit, a big pine branch had fallen on the fence, breaking some wooden battens which normally kept the wire taut, but now it was sagging. She rode Rainbow over and dismounted.

"Perhaps we could jump here."

Looping his reins over the fence, she pulled the broken, rotting branch out of the way.

"It's about shoulder height on you, Rainbow, so that should be okay."

She clambered over the fence and pulled more branches away, so Rainbow had a safe place to land. "That should do it."

She could feel the minutes ticking away as she showed Rainbow the fence and circled him. Perhaps she should have just gone the other way and risked that someone might see her go into the forest without asking permission.

But she was here now, and they simply had to jump the broken fence.

Lily cantered Rainbow at the fence. One, two, three strides and over!

She gasped as the pony stumbled slightly on landing before she managed to turn him away from the trees. He picked his way carefully through the scrub growing between the pines and the fence. Lily asked Rainbow to canter as soon as they reached the track into the pines leading from the locked gate.

"I'm sure this track takes us to the main one, so let's go!"

The rough gravel trail took them across a ridge line then they slowed to go down a hill. "Here's the main track."

Familiar with the road's ups and downs, they cantered quickly through to the gate at Sanderson Road. A swift gallop along the grass verge bought them to the abandoned farm driveway.

She pulled Rainbow up partway across the paddock where the unicorns grazed at night. It was empty.

Her heart sank. "We know they hide in the daytime, Rainbow, but I hoped we'd see some sign of them. Let's look along the edge of the bush."

Lily and Rainbow trotted in and out of the pockets of bush-clad gullies which edged the paddock. At every patch of trees, her hopes lifted. Surely some unicorns would be lying down among the native shrubbery.

But there were no unicorns. Anywhere.

Did Abellona reach them overnight? Could they have been captured?

She choked back a sob.

"No! I don't believe it. We have to keep looking."

They reached the end of the big paddock. Acres and acres of the abandoned farm stretched away into the hills. Clumps of trees and bush were dotted all over. Fences wouldn't stop the herd going wherever they wanted, but Lily and Rainbow would have to go through the gates and search each block of bush. The unicorns could be anywhere.

Lily pulled her phone out of her jeans' pocket. Drat. She didn't have time to search more or she'd never get home for eleven o'clock.

"Oh, Ambrosius, where are you?" she called into the brisk breeze.

But there was no response.

"Come on, Rainbow, we may as well go back." She asked him to walk. "I thought they'd be nearby, but we could look and look, and still not find them." She sniffed as tears pricked her eyes. "I still wouldn't know if they were just hiding or somehow Abellona did reach them. We'll just have to hope they meet us at the gate tonight as planned."

Swiping a tear away, Lily nudged Rainbow into a trot as they crossed the paddock and started down the driveway.

Please be okay, Ambrosius!

Lily trotted Rainbow through the pine forest, not wanting to tire him too much before tonight's long ride moving the unicorns. Well, she hoped that was what they'd be doing.

Over and over, she asked herself, could Abellona have

reached the herd? Was Mikaela's ability to sense the evil witch accurate?

She wiped away more tears.

Please, don't let it be true. They will be safe, resting somewhere I couldn't see.

She couldn't be bothered going home via the hill paddock. If someone in the house saw her coming through the forest gate...well, that was the least of her worries.

Feeling glum, Lily sat in the back seat, trying to message Sasha and Chloe while Liam shouted excitedly from his car-seat as they passed things on the road.

"Truck! Tractor! Car! Beach, beach, beach!"

She felt the most un-beachy she'd ever been in her life. But now she was stuck with playing in the shallows with Liam while Mum went swimming.

"No sign of herd," she tapped on her phone. *"Prob jst hiding smwhre I cdnt see."*

A reply from Sasha pinged back immediately. *"Could be captured!"*

"No sign of fight," Lily tapped, realising the significance of the uninterrupted peace of the abandoned farm. Surely, if Abellona had attacked the herd there, she'd have seen something – ripped up pasture, hoof prints, blood... *"All peaceful and undisturbed."*

Feeling slightly less worried with that realisation, she sent the same messages to Chloe.

"Not conclusive," Sasha replied, *"Im still worried.*

"Me too but trying not to." Lily pressed send as Chloe replied, *"I hope that's a good sign. Wht do you think?"*

"More likely herd is hiding than captured. Hope so anyway."

Mum pulled Lily's door open. "Come on, Lily, we're waiting for you."

"What? Why?" Lily shoved her phone in her backpack and scrambled out of the car.

"We parked and unpacked ages ago."

"You did?" She hadn't noticed, but now saw Liam was strapped into the big-wheeled buggy Mum sometimes took running. Kuia was ready to push it over the sandy path to the beach.

"Beach, beach, beach," Liam repeated.

"We're going, buddy. Lily, carry the blankets." Mum shoved a pile into Lily's arms and picked up a cooler bag of drinks and snacks.

After the usual kerfuffle applying sunscreen to Liam, Mum waded into the sea and waved to Lily standing in the shallows, holding Liam's hand. His bucket and spade were clutched in the other.

"Want to make sandcastles?" she asked, leading him over to Kuia sitting on the blanket.

"Yes!" Liam shouted, running ahead.

The sun was much warmer then when she'd been riding earlier, so she pulled off her t-shirt. She had her swimsuit on underneath. "Can you put sunscreen on my back please, Kuia? You dig here, Liam, that's nice firm sand to make a pretty sandcastle for Kuia."

Worried as she was about the unicorns, Lily figured there wasn't much she could do now so decided to build a sandcastle to rival Liam's.

CHAPTER TWELVE

Waiting by the barn, Lily flinched at the tiny clink of metal on metal.

"Sorry," hissed Chloe as she appeared out of the night. "I tried to be so careful with the gate latch too."

Lily grabbed Chloe's hand. "Come on. I stashed our tack under the trees in the horse paddock again. Sasha is meeting us there."

The crunch of their steady footsteps on the gravel yards around the barn sounded awfully loud in the still, cool night.

A morepork's simple call made them both jump. Lily huffed out a breath of relief when they got through the gate into the horse paddock and could walk quietly on the grass. "Gee, it's awful, this sneaking out at night, isn't it? I've never been so worried in all my life."

"I reckon," Chloe whispered. "My heart was beating so loud as I went past Mum's room, I was sure she'd be able to hear it." She stumbled over a clump of grass. "Oof! Mum's been asking some funny questions."

"Like what?"

"Like have I heard any noises in the night or noticed the back door was unlocked?"

"Oh, help..."

"Come on, you two!" Sasha's voice hissed from the gloom by the trees.

"Ooh..." Chloe gasped, her hand clutching at Lily's. "I didn't expect you to be here yet."

"Ambrosius said an hour before moonrise, didn't he?" Sasha sounded anxious. "And we checked the moon chart together, so I'm here and you both need to hurry up! The ponies are standing together around here."

As quickly as she could, Lily put Rainbow's bridle and saddle on. The pony snorted, shifting as she pulled the girth up. "Steady, boy, you're excited about these night rides now, aren't you?"

Sasha swung up into Tommy's saddle. "He's not excited, just worried we're not going to find the unicorns tonight, that they've been captured," she said angrily.

Lily bit her lip. There was no point snapping back at Sasha. They were just as worried as each other. Checking Chloe was okay, she mounted Rainbow and leaned down to check the girth. "We better get moving then. The sooner we reach the farm, the sooner we'll know."

Sasha pushed Tommy into a trot as soon as they were clear of the trees. The night was dark, and the ponies followed the familiar route to the forest gate without any problems.

"Sigvard!" Sasha exclaimed in a kind of whispered shout as they caught sight of the big unicorn.

Lily felt a surge of excitement. "He's here! I hope that means that the herd is alright."

Sasha flung herself off Tommy and over the gate to wrap her arms around Sigvard's neck. "Are you okay?"

"Yes, we are. We have rested, Brökk says he's nearly back to full strength and now Ambrosius is anxious to move, so let us hurry."

Sasha bustled everyone through the gate and secured the latch. "Any sign of Abellona?"

"Mikaela says she senses her much more strongly now." His voice was factual, resolute. "She must be close."

Lily's stomach clenched. *This is it. We are definitely helping the unicorns to move tonight.*

"Do you need the glow?" asked Sigvard. "I would prefer not to show any light if we can."

"I think the ponies will be okay if we stick together," said Sasha. "What do you think?" She looked at the others.

Lily nodded, too anxious to speak.

"I guess so," said Chloe, her face pale and scared in the faint light from the stars.

"Then let's go." The unicorn cantered off along the track, Sasha and Tommy right beside him. Lily and Chloe followed close behind, but they'd only gone a few metres before Chloe waved her arm at Lily.

"I have to stop." She clutched her mouth and slipped from Angel's back before stumbling to the edge of the track.

"Wait!" Lily called to the others.

"What?" said Sasha.

"It's Chloe," said Lily as she caught Angel's loose reins. She heard Chloe being sick. "Are you okay, Chlo'?"

"Um, I think so." She came around her pony. "I guess it's nerves."

"I know how you feel." Lily slipped off Rainbow. "I'll give you a leg-up."

"Thanks. Actually, I feel better now."

"Good," came the unicorn's rumbling voice. "Ambrosius awaits!"

Sigvard plunged off into the night, and Lily let Rainbow spring forward after him and her friends. No one wanted to get left behind in the dark.

Cantering up a hill towards a clearing in the pines, Lily had an awful sensation they were being followed.

She glanced round.

Oh no!

The words froze in her throat.

Something black and winged broke the star-lit night sky high above them.

Anchoring her hands against Rainbow's saddle as he cantered fast with the others, Lily turned her body to get a better look.

One large flying creature. About the size of a pegasus.

It could be Guilio.

Oh, there was something on the pegasus's back. And several smaller flying creatures around it.

A cold fear washed over her, leaving her weak and desperately hanging onto her pony.

Their worst nightmare.

"Abellona!" she managed to croak.

Sigvard didn't hesitate, plunging off the track into the pines. The ponies followed, stumbling over old tree stumps and scrub as they tried to keep up with the bigger unicorn.

Lily's heart pounded. Oh god. What if a pony caught a leg in a rabbit hole? She didn't know whether to slow Rainbow or trust he could see much better than she could. It was terrifying!

"Sigvard, wait!" she called.

Instantly, the unicorn spun to face her. The ponies didn't need to be told to stop. They were all breathing hard.

Lily tried to catch her breath. "It's Abellona, isn't it?"

"Yes." Sigvard scanned the sky through the trees overhead.

Chloe gasped. "Oh, no!"

"We've got to keep going, to tell the herd," Sasha shouted hoarsely.

"We all need to keep going," he replied briskly. "But they'll know. Guilio should have got through with a message from Mikaela well before Abellona came out of the chasm."

"Um," Chloe squeaked, "if you're here, was Mikaela alone on the beach?"

"No." Sigvard snapped his gaze to Chloe, then back to the sky. "Fredek and Isak, my next in command, were on guard. All three will have made their way back to the herd as soon as they were sure when Abellona would arrive."

"But what if none of them managed to reach the herd?" Lily's stomach clenched again, and she had to swallow hard to stop being sick. "What if Ambrosius doesn't know? You must go, Sigvard! And fast! The ponies will help us find the herd, I'm sure, if you move from the farm."

Sigvard shook his head, his mane flying impatiently. "We all go. Together. Ambrosius said I was to bring you safely to him. I can't leave you here with *her* hunting overhead."

"But surely she's looking for unicorns, not humans," Sasha said. "You're in more danger out here, away from the herd, than we are."

The warrior unicorn snorted. "I've fought Abellona before and won, believe me!"

"Sigvard, please, just go," Lily begged. "The herd needs you. We'll be okay."

"Go!" Sasha shouted again.

The dark grey unicorn looked at Sasha, his eyes

worried. "I do not like leaving you against Ambrosius's orders."

"We know, but Ambrosius needs you more than we do." Sasha reached out to smooth the wild curls of his forelock out of his eyes. "We'll follow, keeping watch carefully all the way."

"Very carefully." Sigvard rubbed his cheek on Sasha's hand.

"Of course."

Tears pricked Lily's eyes. The unicorns meant so much to them now. She'd do anything to help keep them safe.

Sigvard spun on his hocks and disappeared into the darkness.

They were alone in the forest. Lily shivered as an icy chill trickled down her neck. Somewhere in the skies above, a demented witch was trying to track down and capture their unicorn friends.

"I'm frightened," Chloe whispered.

"Me too." Lily grabbed Chloe's hand and squeezed. "But I trust the ponies will follow Sigvard's path somehow and lead us to the herd. Come on."

She pointed Rainbow in the direction Sigvard had gone and the others followed.

"Have we done the right thing," Chloe called in a hushed voice, "sending Sigvard away?"

"Of course we have." Lily leaned back as Rainbow scrambled down a small bank onto what looked like a rough track. "Making sure the herd knows Abellona is here is the most important thing. As Sasha said, she's hunting for unicorns, not people."

"Are you sure?" Chloe's voice quavered. "Maybe Abellona would just kill us so she can go after the unicorns. What if she captured us to try and entrap the unicorns?"

"Stop it!" Lily watched Chloe and Angel stumble down the bank. "You're making me really scared now. We've *got* to find the herd and see if we can help."

"But should we even go near the herd, if that's where *she* is?"

"Chloe!" Sasha and Tommy pulled up. "How could you say that? How can we leave them now? Don't you want to make sure Mikaela is alright?"

"Of course, but I'm worried we'll be more of a hazard than a help," Chloe replied as they set off along the rutted track in a steady trot. "What if there's some kind of fight? It's not like we can fight alongside them."

Lily had been wondering much the same herself but recalled what Ambrosius had said. "If they decide to move, we can help keep the foals together in groups the way Ambrosius asked us to do. And we know the roads to take if they want to go to the big park."

"I agree with Lily," Sasha said, pushing Tommy into a canter as the track suddenly turned onto a dirt road that seemed to take them in the right direction, "and we can't leave you to turn home by yourself, so you'll have to come with us."

Sasha's words were like her normal bossy self, but Lily could hear her voice tremble with worry.

"It's not like I don't want to help, Sash." Chloe raised her voice to carry over the thud of hooves. "And I didn't mean we should go home, we have to find the herd, but I don't want us to be more of a problem for the unicorns than a help."

"We'll figure out whether we can help when we find them. But first, let's find them." Sasha led the way along the road which bought them to the gate at the end of Sanderson Road from a different direction.

"Good. We know where we are now." She leaned down to open the gate.

"Wait!" Lily said quietly. "Should we be going this way? We'll be out in the open going up the drive."

"Good point." Sasha looked around. "If we ride along the fence that way, we'll be nearer the gully paddock where the unicorns are."

"But how will we get over the fence?" Chloe followed Sasha as Tommy scrambled over a fallen log against the fence.

"We'll figure it out when we get there."

"I hate to think how scratched the ponies' legs are after pushing through all that scrub," Lily grumbled when they reached a big gully which ran down from the unicorns' paddock into the forest.

"Do you think the unicorns were somewhere close to the top of this gully?" Sasha stopped Tommy and looked.

"I think so," said Lily. "That's where the grass was most crushed when I came this afternoon."

"Okay, let's see where we can get over the fence." Sasha walked Tommy carefully down the darkened slope under overhanging trees.

Angel didn't want to follow Tommy. "Come on, girl. You're okay." Chloe tried to kick her on.

"Hey, guys! The fence is down." Sasha's voice was loud in the still night air. "Looks like it's been trampled by the unicorns."

"Ssshh!" Lily hissed, pushing Rainbow into Angel to force her to move. "Keep your voice down!"

"Sorry!" Sasha whispered when they reached her. "But

look! All the posts are pushed over, and rocks placed on the wires here so the ponies can walk across it safely."

"Weird." Lily looked around. No human would leave a paddock fence like this. The unicorns must have done it. But how did they move the rocks?

"Come on." Sasha walked Tommy over the flattened fence.

Lily hung back in case Angel was spooky about this unexpected obstacle, but she followed Tommy with no problem. "Can you hear something? Hoof beats, maybe?" She pulled Rainbow up beside the others.

"Yes, just up the gully. Come on!"

"Carefully, Sash, carefully!" Lily whispered as her impatient friend trotted off.

CHAPTER THIRTEEN

L ily and Rainbow crested the lip of the gully just in time to see Sasha galloping Tommy at Ambrosius and Sigvard.

The unicorns faced each other, heads down, looking like they might charge. The curves of their spikes glinted in the moonlight as the herd around them watched.

"Oh, no!" Lily pushed Rainbow to follow Sasha. "What's happening?"

Ambrosius looked around as she neared. "He left you alone in the forest. That's one thing." He shook his head with a big snort. "And the other thing is we can't agree whether to move as one group or split up."

"We told Sigvard to go, Ambrosius." Lily urged Rainbow closer to the silver unicorn. "It was more important that you knew Abellona flew over us."

"Mikaela reported her arrival some time ago."

"We thought Mikaela would be on to it, but we wanted to be sure that you definitely knew."

The unicorn king nodded in acknowledgement and

looked back to his lieutenant. "We move now as one group. Get the herd organised."

"I will say it one more time, Sire, travelling in smaller groups makes it easier to hide. If *she* tracks us, the other groups may be able to make a surprise attack to help the other."

"It spreads our resources too thinly," Ambrosius countered quickly. "We don't yet have another sensory of Mikaela's capability. We only have one Brökk. How is he to be split between groups? Your guard is light in number and experience, as you yourself acknowledge."

"True, Sire, but I speak from bitter experience, as you well know," the big unicorn said respectfully.

"Yes, Sigvard," Ambrosius replied with a short sigh. "I recall clearly the day Abellona ambushed us. The day we lost many valued members of your guard and Viveka."

Lily swallowed. How awful.

"But," Ambrosius continued, "I lead this herd, and in the interest of speed, we must all leave as one group and now! Mikaela, an update please."

"She's someway inland, Sire. Over to the east."

"Thank you. Let us move! Quickly!"

"Finally," Sasha whispered to Lily, as Sigvard neighed loudly several times and the herd gathered into a tight group. "I can't believe they're arguing when they should be moving. They should have moved ages ago."

"I know. It doesn't make any sense," Lily whispered back.

Chloe leaned in. "I wonder if they would be best to stay here now. She's more likely to see them on the road, isn't she?"

Lily looked at Chloe, her eyes wide and worried. "Oh, you're might be right, Chlo. It's too late to suggest..."

"Lily!" Ambrosius's voice rolled out. "I want you in the lead with me. Chloe will ride with Mikaela and Brökk with half the warrior guard at the rear. Sasha will be with Sigvard, Fredek and Isak, and the rest of the guard, helping keep everyone together and moving as fast as the foals can manage. Guilio will maintain his usual overhead guard."

Everyone moved to their positions.

"Forward!" commanded Ambrosius.

The thunder of hundreds of hooves shook the ground as Lily cantered beside Ambrosius, who seemed to be looking everywhere at once.

"Keep Rainbow to a steady canter," he instructed. "That's a good speed for the foals."

The herd surged across the big paddock and down the drive of the abandoned farm. Lily turned back, trying to see Chloe and Sasha, but they were lost among the flashing unicorn spikes and movement of many bodies.

"Wow..." The sight was amazing.

"Lily!" Ambrosius' voice brought her attention back. "We turn left onto the road, correct?"

"Yes." She slowed Rainbow for the turn, an eager foal pushing between them and the gatepost. A sharp nip from Ambrosius sent the foal back to its mother.

"Keep to the side of the road where you can." The unicorn matched his pace to Rainbow's. "Use every over-hanging tree. The others will follow."

Sanderson Road wound through hills as it headed towards the highway, almost looping back on itself as it crossed a small river to the south of the farm.

Without warning, Ambrosius swerved left onto the gravel riverbank. Heart thumping in time with the thundering hoof-beats, Lily followed. "Where are you going?" she shouted.

"Mikaela sent me a silent message." He didn't slow. "Abellona is close! Aim for those trees on the right."

"Run, Rainbow, run!" Lily leaned forward, urging her pony over the loose gravel, which seemed to suck his speed with every slithering step.

She glanced behind. Some of the herd were still turning off the road. She saw Sasha and Sigvard standing in the middle of the road to make sure everyone turned. They all had a way to go to reach the trees.

I hope Chloe is okay! She's right at the back with Brökk.

At last Rainbow plunged into the relative darkness of the trees.

Ambrosius wheeled. "Stand on the edge here to show the others where to head. Tell them to stay close. I'm going back to make sure everyone's safely off the road."

Trembling with fright, Lily positioned Rainbow where she was told. The pony sucked in deep breaths as unicorns charged into the trees. "Stay near! Don't go too far away!" she called again and again.

Anxious whinnies sounded out as mothers called to keep their foals close by in the dense stand of trees. Sweaty unicorns puffed after the frightening dash to the trees.

Straining to see in the silvery haze of moonlight, Lily looked and looked for Chloe's palomino mare, Brökk's dark coat or Mikaela's distinctive silver and black markings.

More foals and their anxious mothers joined the group under the trees.

"There they are!" Lily told Rainbow. "Thank goodness. That means everyone's off the road now."

Sigvard and Sasha swung in behind Chloe and the others, Guilio wheeling overhead. Ambrosius moved up and down the river's edge, urging the mares and foals on.

A bolt of fire suddenly shot from the sky, lighting up the

riverbank before sizzling into the river right beside Ambrosius. He screamed a warning neigh, and the herd continued to surge into the trees as Guilio flew backwards and forwards overhead.

"Come on!" Lily shouted to Sasha and Sigvard, who accompanied the last few mares with the smallest foals, darling Lief among them.

Brökk and Ambrosius halted, breathing hard, near Lily. Chloe bought a steaming Angel to stand beside Lily.

Then she saw another mighty pegasus clear against the inky black of the night sky.

It was Galen, Guilio's brother.

On his back was a dark, robed creature, watching the unicorns gather in the trees.

"Abell..." The sorceress' name froze in her throat, and all she wanted to do was bury her face in Rainbow's mane and shut out the sight of the witch who persecuted the unicorns for her own warped reasons. But she felt compelled to watch as the witch directed Galen closer and closer.

Their worst fears had come true.

Abellona had found the herd.

There was nowhere to run.

Snap! Boom! Abellona's next strike smashed down right in front of them.

Rainbow jumped back as Lily tried not to scream.

The gravel riverbank offered nothing for the fire to burn, and the flames puffed out into smoke.

"Hold your fire," Ambrosius said to Brökk, who seemed to sparkle with magical energy. "Save your strength until she's close enough to hurt seriously."

Lily felt the witch's gaze pass over her. Then their eyes

met. The witch's dark eyes were compelling, holding hers captive for a long moment while the witch probed...

"Yuck, no!" Lily snapped her eyes shut. It felt like Abellona was searching her *mind* via her eyes. Horrible! She shuddered. *Never, ever look at her directly again*, she told herself.

Abellona pointed her long staff at the last group racing for the trees.

Bang!

The fire bolt touched down, and a foal squealed. Flames flared from its back briefly before it crumpled to the ground.

Sigvard neighed frantically as he and Tommy stood over the foal, its fearful mother not leaving its side.

Sasha shook her fist at the witch and shouted, "We'll get you for that!"

"Sasha looks angry," Lily said to Chloe. "No witch is going to hurt her precious Sigvard."

"I'd be terrified out there," Chloe whispered. "I am terrified anyway."

"Me too. How are the unicorns going to stop her now?"

The girls clutched hands as Abellona fired again, striking the ground close to Tommy, driving him back from the foal.

Another strike. Sigvard stepped back.

Bang! The mare retreated briefly.

The fire bolts kept coming, fast.

Ambrosius spoke with Brökk, their words barely audible to Lily over the crack of each bolt. She caught "not close enough" and "only just strong enough". She hadn't had the chance to ask today if Brökk felt back to full strength. How were they going to fight Abellona without him?

Sasha edged Tommy closer to the foal huddled on the

ground. It didn't look like she or any of the others would abandon it. She stood in her stirrups and yelled, "Help!"

Lily shouted at Ambrosius. "We have to get the foal back here." She looked back at the sky. Abellona had wheeled Galen even closer, fire crackling down around the foal as Sigvard and Tommy frantically dodged each attack.

"Oh, God," Chloe sobbed. "How can we help?"

Brökk stepped forward, swung his head, and *wham*...! A brilliant flash of light shot from his ivory spike. It hit Abellona's shoulder in a shower of sparks. The witch screamed angrily, obviously hurt, but wheeled Galen higher.

"She's out of reach again, Sire." Brökk shook his head, frustrated. "Her firepower is stronger than mine. It always has been."

The witch's fire bolts continued, making Sigvard and Tommy leap and dodge.

Lily didn't know whether to be more worried about Sasha and Tommy or the unicorns.

"Can we lift the foal between us?" She looked at Chloe.

"I don't know!" Chloe's eyes were wide with fear. "The three of us probably could."

Lily turned to Ambrosius and Brökk. "We have to get to the foal and carry him back!" It didn't matter how frightened she was, she couldn't leave the foal to be killed.

"I can't let you do that, Lily," Ambrosius shook his head. "If we give little Cosme enough time and protect him from more injuries, I hope he can get up himself very soon."

"Why are you saying that?" Lily stifled a sob. Surely Ambrosius wouldn't sacrifice the foal. "He's hurt! How can you expect him to run?"

"Sometimes it's the way of the world." The unicorn king spoke with great sadness. "We can't always rescue our injured."

"Can't Brökk magic him back?" Lily asked, desperate for a solution.

Cosme gave a shrill whinny, fearful and frightened, while neither senior unicorn answered.

"You can create a great chasm through the earth, but you can't move a little foal from just over there?" Lily raged at Brökk, who looked at Ambrosius, his eyes bleak.

Then, from above, came the heart-stopping sound of Abellona's voice. "I shall take this youngster, Ambrosius, and teach him to respect his betters."

The sorceress' voice was creepily quiet yet cut like a sharp blade.

Lily whipped her hands over her ears, but it was still distressingly audible when Abellona added, "Yes, teach him to respect me. That's what I'll do. Just like I did with Isak and Ragnor, and of course dear Galen here who carries me tonight."

Ambrosius flinched as the witch said each name.

Fear of what Abellona had done to those poor captured unicorns made Lily's stomach heave as she watched Sigvard and others constantly circling the stricken foal, dodging to draw Abellona's fire bolts away from him.

How one of them hadn't been hit, Lily couldn't imagine.

"Lily! Chloe!" Sasha yelled. "We have to do something!"

Lily swallowed down that fear. They did have to do something if the unicorns couldn't. Even if she didn't know how they could get to Cosme and back without being hurt – or worse.

"We're coming!" she yelled. To Chloe she said, "Do we ride the ponies out and risk them getting hurt while we carry the foal back? Or run out? Which will be slower?"

"We ride." Chloe looked determined as she shoved her riding helmet tightly on her head. "As fast as we can."

"Wait!" Brökk commanded. "I will try a protective spell. It may work."

"No," snapped Ambrosius. "Think of the greater good. Conserve your powers. Look! Cosme is trying to stand."

The foal struggled, his legs flailing. Then he slumped down.

"No, Ambrosius," said Brökk. "Lily is right. Every foal is precious."

"Of course they are," Ambrosius spoke quickly. "But I must think of the herd, and we need you as strong as possible. We have the battle of our lives ahead tonight. You know that."

"I do," Brökk agreed. "But think of morale. To save Cosme from enslavement would boost the herd, to show them it is possible to succeed over Abellona."

A mare standing near the girls whispered, "We've never, ever managed to get anyone back once they've been captured."

"Oh, God!" Lily breathed, hoping Ambrosius would agree to the rescue attempt. She swallowed hard against the cold fear that crept up her throat.

The unicorn king nodded.

"Girls, come here." Brökk spoke urgently.

Lily and Chloe turned their ponies to the mage. Brökk touched his horn to Rainbow's nose and then Angel's. A milky cloud encompassed the ponies and the girls. "Go!"

They galloped straight for Cosme, the ponies straining across the shifting gravel. The eerie glow stretched from the tip of Brökk's horn around them both as they ran.

Lily assumed the cloud was a kind of shield, but she

didn't have time to think. The faster they could rescue Cosme, the less magic Brökk would have to use.

Abellona struck with bright lightning.

Lily flinched, but the bolt glanced off the milky cloud, deflected into the night sky.

"Thank God," Chloe panted as they reached the group clustered around Cosme.

The cloud expanded to surround them all.

Oh, clever Brökk! The thought raced through Lily's mind as she flung herself off Rainbow.

The next bolt from Abellona ricocheted away just as harmlessly. *The shield is working!*

An angry cry from above sounded as Chloe and Sasha landed beside her, the ponies left to fend for themselves. She had to trust they could dodge Abellona's bolts as successfully as the others had managed or stay close by under the shield.

Poor Cosme was badly burned.

"How do we carry him?" Chloe crouched down by Cosme's head to pat him. "Thank goodness he's one of the smallest."

"You take his shoulders and neck, Chlo," Lily puffed. "Sasha, take his rump. I'll lift in the middle and hope I don't hurt his burn too much."

"Better a bit hurt, than captured," Sasha said as she put one arm under the foal's flank, the other around his long legs. "Okay, one, two, three!"

They lifted and stood for a second as Chloe adjusted her hold so Cosme's head was comfortable.

"Oof," Lily panted. "He might be one of the smallest, but he's plenty solid."

Sasha grunted as she shifted her hold. "Okay, we're walking."

"Come on, ponies." Lily clicked her tongue. Sigvard, the mare and the ponies stayed within the cloud as they trudged step by terrifying step across the lumpy gravel riverbank.

Chloe flinched every time Abellona struck the shield. "I'm trying to ignore the witch chucking fire bolts at us, but it's not easy!"

"Let's hope Brökk can maintain this spell until we reach the trees." Lily would have crossed her fingers if she could.

Sigvard and the others walked in a semi-circle right behind them to keep the shield as small as possible. Rainbow's breath was hot on her neck, and she was glad to have him near.

Each metre of their journey seemed to take forever. Thank goodness Cosme stayed still and didn't struggle, but Lily's shoulders ached with the foal's weight. Her arms were under his tummy, meaning her face was close to his burnt back. She felt sick from the smell of charred flesh, but that wasn't going to stop her now.

She watched the milky cloud in front of them, how it stretched all the way back to Brökk at the edge of the trees. It seemed to hold steady.

Until a particularly bright fire bolt sizzled into the edge of the cloud.

"The shield! It's fractured!" Lily couldn't point. "On the left."

Sasha cursed under her breath. "Can you guys go any faster?"

"Not really," Chloe panted.

"That's okay. Just keep going, step by step." Lily watched the fractured point of the shield. "It's not growing, the broken bit. It's sort of moving ahead of us as we get closer."

"You're doing well," Sigvard said from Sasha's shoulder. "Not far now."

Abellona struck again with a red-tinged bolt.

The milky glow of the shield faded away to nothing. A chilling laugh drifted out of the sky, and Lily saw Abellona circle Galen for another strike.

CHAPTER FOURTEEN

"Oh, no!" Chloe gasped. "I'll try to run. Come on!"
Stumbling in the heavy gravel and joggling poor Cosme, they ran. Sigvard and the ponies spread out to protect them as best they could.

Lily had her eyes fixed on the safety of the trees. It was horrible, trying to run without being able to see where her feet were going. And the burnt flesh smell. The witch overhead, poised to strike.

Lily gasped for breath, then stumbled, letting go of Cosme as she tried to regain her balance.

Sasha swore loudly as she and Chloe sagged, nearly dropping the foal.

Puffing, Lily took her share of Cosme's weight again. "Sorry!"

In front, Rainbow trotted beside Sigvard, constantly weaving to try and upset Abellona's aim.

But it didn't work. Rainbow squealed as a streak of fire carved across his rump just as he and Sigvard reached the trees.

Lily gasped as the fire bolt turned into a sudden ball of flame, engulfing the tree closest to Rainbow.

"Go left!" Lily shouted as they swerved away from the burning tree. "Come on, Rainbow!"

They managed a few metres into the trees before Chloe sagged to the ground. "We did it!" She burst into tears. "I've never been so frightened in all my life."

Sasha wrapped one arm around Chloe, her other hand gripping Lily's. "We did do it. We saved Cosme from Abellona."

Lily wiped sweat from her face. "I can't believe it." She turned to Brökk. "The shield worked. Thank you."

"We're not free yet," the mage replied with a tired sigh as he pointed his spike towards the burning tree. A cloud appeared directly over it, then a downpour of rain put the fire out in seconds before the cloud puffed out of existence.

Lily grinned. "That's a handy spell to know."

"Especially as fire is her favourite way to flush unicorns or whoever she's chasing out of hiding."

Oh. Brökk's bald statement wiped the smile from Lily's face as Abellona's fire bolts continued to rain down, though more slowly.

"Does she ever get tired?"

"She draws her strength from the creatures she has enslaved. We don't know how long poor Galen will survive, the way she drives him such long distances while also sucking the limited magical powers of a pegasus."

Lily crouched beside Cosme's head, stroking his neck. She looked up at the unicorn king, standing silently nearby. He looked so stricken, like he didn't have any fight left in him. It didn't feel right. Surely Ambrosius wouldn't have brought his herd to the other side of the world to just give in now?

"What are you going to do, Ambrosius?"

He replied with a question of his own. "Can you help Cosme? His mother, Zivena, is obviously worried."

"Of course. I have some burn balm in Rainbow's saddle bag."

"I'll get it for you, Lil." Sasha had made sure the ponies were okay. "Shall I put some on Rainbow's rump as well?"

"Oh, yes!" Lily jumped up. "My poor pony, I'm sorry!" She was so worried about the unicorns. Especially Ambrosius who was walking along the edge of the trees away from the herd. "Chloe, can you apply the balm to Cosme? I want to talk with Ambrosius for a minute."

She scrambled after the unicorn king. After a few minutes he stopped, turning to look up at the sky.

Lily reached a hand out to Ambrosius, and he sniffed it, just like Rainbow or any horse would. "What's wrong, Ambrosius?"

"What's right?" he countered as she came close to hug his neck.

"What do you mean?" She stepped back to look him in the eye.

"Nothing is right, is it? We were meant to escape Abellona. To make a fresh start. To give the herd a chance to rebuild our strength, train new warriors for Sigvard's guard. Then go back and free Celestina."

"But you always thought she would follow you. Didn't your plan include how to counter her?"

"I hoped we'd have more time. None of us realised Brökk would be so badly affected by bringing a chasm this far."

Lily sighed. "I know, but Brökk is much better now, isn't he?" She ran a hand down his silky cheek.

"Thankfully yes, but every bit of magic he uses seems to take longer to be replenished."

Lily tilted her head, trying to understand. "Kind of like a well or pool of water. If you use some, you have to wait for more water to trickle in?"

"Something like that." The unicorn stepped forward to look up at the sky.

"So what now?" Lily also looked up. The brilliance of the Milky Way overhead was uninterrupted.

"She'll be back. Soon probably. With her army. They'll be near somewhere. We'll fight. And we'll see who's the victor in the end."

Chill fear swept through her at his words. He sounded so resigned. Like they'd lose, as they had previously.

Not if I can help it.

Lily took a steadying breath. "You haven't come all the way to my country to give up now, you know."

The unicorn looked at her. "Lily, I appreciate your words of encouragement, but we know our enemy, and you do not."

Ideas bounced around in her head. "I know you know her. That's what I'm counting on. Come on!" She scrambled up on a fallen log beside Ambrosius and clambered on his back. "Take me back to the others. Let's come up with a plan. Isn't attack the best form of defence?"

The unicorn carried her without comment, jumping gracefully over logs and weaving through the trees.

Hands wrapped in Ambrosius's long, curly mane, Lily lost herself in the absolute delight of actually riding the unicorn.

Oh. My. God.

"Lily! You're riding Ambrosius!" Sasha shrieked, bringing Lily back to reality.

The herd could be under attack any minute. "Sigvard, Brökk!" Lily called. "Mikaela!" She stayed on Ambrosius's back as the others gathered round. The warmth from his body on her legs in the cool of the night was welcome.

"Ambrosius said something that sparked an idea. You know Abellona." She looked around the group. "What are her weaknesses? What can we do that might weaken her? You said she draws magical power from other creatures like Galen. Can we stop that somehow?"

"You wouldn't want to harm Galen though," Chloe said.

"Of course not," Lily agreed. "Is there some way to give Galen the strength to fight Abellona's power over him? Would that be enough?"

Ambrosius lifted his head. "We need to free Xanthe," he said quietly.

"Yes!" Sigvard replied in a hushed and excited tone. "If we free Xanthe, Galen will also be freed from Abellona's spell. He will then bring her to us."

"Perfect!" Sasha reached up to high five Lily.

Lily felt a buzz of excitement. "So how do we find Xanthe?" *Could this plan work?*

Mikaela spoke, "I will search. Abellona will have a temporary camp nearby, somewhere between here and the chasm. Xanthe and her guards always travel with Abellona and Galen."

"I will help you." Guilio's serious voice came from among the trees.

"How do you stop Abellona from attacking whoever goes to look for Xanthe?" Chloe asked.

"We create a distraction. We engage her in battle," responded Sigvard, pawing the ground eagerly.

Lily shivered at the very thought. She knew they were

battle-hardened warriors, but she hated the idea they might get hurt.

The ponies might get hurt too. Or us.

Another shiver ran down her body as cold fear crept around her neck and clutched at her throat.

"The thing is," Ambrosius's deep voice broke into her thoughts, "I do not know by what means Xanthe is kept captive, but I feel sure human hands are more use than a unicorn's spike for that job."

Lily swallowed. "So you want us to go with Mikaela and Guilio?"

"I feel stealth is of vital importance, so just one of you. Angel's colouring makes her too obvious..."

"I want to fight alongside Sigvard," Sasha interrupted. "I must be able to help somehow."

Lily slid off Ambrosius's back, her legs feeling weak. "Which leaves me and Rainbow," she whispered.

The unicorn king looked at her solemnly. "Will you do it? Everyone else will either be keeping the foals safe or fighting for our lives."

She looked up into his eyes.

He was counting on her.

Her head nodded before she'd properly formed the thought of agreeing.

"Excellent." Ambrosius rubbed his cheek on her shoulder and, absently, she patted him. "I ask that Mikaela and Guilio return here as soon as you have a clear direction.

I've got to free the imprisoned pegasus.

By myself.

She felt numb.

"Great plan," Sigvard said. "Mikaela, Guilio, Lily. You'll need a head start, so go as soon as possible. We won't be able to hold her off for very long if she and her army are fighting at full strength."

"I'm feeling strong, much stronger tonight," Brökk interrupted. "Perhaps it's because there's more magic close by."

"Excellent, Brökk," said Ambrosius. "Just what I wanted to hear. Lily, stay with us as long as possible. It's safer. As soon as Mikaela has fixed the position of Abellona's camp, she can start back. Guilio will be faster so he can return, then accompany Lily back to that location."

Oh boy...

Lily's heart pounded and she tried to breath, but she couldn't.

Sasha whacked her on the back. "Lily! You okay?"

"Arhh," she gasped, then coughed. "Think so, but crazy frightened. Aren't you?"

"Yes, but excited. We're going to beat Abellona this time. I just know it."

"Right." Ambrosius spoke decisively. "To draw Abellona into battle, we will go back along the road towards the farm a short distance. The movement will catch her attention, but we should reach a very dense stand of trees near a large flat paddock before she mobilises her bewitched troops. Our mares and foals can be in the trees, and we have a clear view to the road and over the forest on the other side. Brökk can easily throw spells, and it's only a small area of trees if he needs to shield. Mikaela, Guilio, do you know where I mean? Can you find it?"

"Yes, Sire," they both replied.

"Excellent, then be on your way. And good luck!" He raised his voice slightly. "Form up! Drink quickly at the river as we pass. Let's move!"

The thunder of hooves and pounding of hearts

drummed all thought from Lily's mind as she raced Rainbow along the riverbank beside Sasha and Chloe.

They paused briefly for the ponies to drink, the herd's mage drinking beside them.

Then on to the road, they swiftly reached the place Ambrosius intended for them to stand and fight the herd's evil enemy.

Lily's heart thumped as Ambrosius and Sigvard issued instructions. "Mares and foals into the trees. Young guards defending on the edge of the trees. Warriors, form up in front of the guard! Brökk, what do you think of this as a defensive position?"

Lily joined Sasha and Chloe with the warriors. Chloe's face was deathly pale in the moonlight when Lily glanced at her friends.

Sasha's eyes were bright as she looked around. "Magnificent, aren't they?" she whispered to Lily over the restless movement of the warrior unicorns.

Lily nodded, too overwhelmed to speak.

They didn't know when Abellona might strike.

She had no idea what or who made up Abellona's enslaved army.

What creatures they would be facing.

Or how she was going to free Xanthe...

"Girls!" Ambrosius called. "Find a strong stick. You're going to need some kind of weapon. But stay here with the younger guard in defence."

"Oh, God," Chloe whimpered. "I can't believe this is happening."

"You stay with me," Sasha said. "I'll look after you."

They scrambled off the ponies and rummaged in the undergrowth.

"She comes!" Sigvard called, as he and many others consistently scanned the starlit skies above. "To the west."

Lily's heart thudded as she leapt onto Rainbow again, a jagged, broken-off manuka branch in her hand.

Galen, carrying his vile captor, soared into sight. Around them appeared dozens of flying creatures.

"Rocs," said Ambrosius, who moved to stand beside Lily. "Giant birds of prey."

She shivered. They were huge, nearly as big as the pegasus.

"What are the others?" She spoke quietly in the awful silence, which fell as the herd watched their enemy approach.

"Zilants carrying giant fighting cats. And probably her combat dog squad."

She gulped.

"What," Sasha's hushed voice trembled, "is a zilant?"

"A winged snake with the head of a dragon."

"And you've fought these creatures before and survived?" Sasha looked at Ambrosius.

"We have," he stated solemnly. "We haven't won, but we have survived to fight another day."

"Today we win!" Sasha whispered fiercely.

"Today we win!" Sigvard echoed his human friend in his booming voice.

"Today we win!" The herd shouted as one.

Abellona's forces closed on the vast flat paddock before them.

"Hold your positions," Ambrosius instructed.

"That's right," Brökk said. "Draw them in. As close as you dare so I can hit Abellona directly."

Rainbow shifted nervously under Lily. "It's alright, pony," she said, running a soothing hand down his neck, her eyes locked on Galen and the figure on his back.

Abellona raised her arm, pointing her long staff directly at their group. A green glow swirled around her hands.

"Be ready," Ambrosius said to Brökk.

A fire bolt exploded from the witch's staff towards them. *Boom!*

Brökk intercepted with a lightning-fast raincloud. The fire bolt sizzled out harmlessly before it reached them.

"Yay!" Sasha shouted.

Bang. Abellona fired again.

Boom. Brökk responded.

The unicorns stood steadfast in formation as Galen carried Abellona closer.

"Steady," Ambrosius said to Brökk.

"I've got it," the mage replied.

He judged the distance perfectly, sending a flash of white lightning from his ivory spike. The bolt smashed into Abellona's shoulder.

Her magical staff plummeted to earth with a thud as she shrieked at her fighters. "Dive! Full attack!"

The zilants flew close to the ground, the giant fighting cats leaping down before the winged serpents swept up to join the rocs. As one, the cats ran full pelt at the herd.

"Now!" Sigvard yelled.

And the unicorns charged, heads lowered at the enormous snarling cats. Sasha galloped Tommy beside Sigvard.

"Sasha, no!" Lily screamed. *She's meant to stay with Chloe and me!*

The combined roc and zilant flight dive-bombed the unicorns, deadly claws raking and ripping. Screams of pain and anger rang out as Abellona shrieked more instructions. Sasha and Tommy were in there somewhere.

There!

Lily saw Sasha smash her stick up into a roc's belly. It slumped to the ground, where Sigvard ran it through with his spike.

"Do we help?" she asked Chloe.

"I don't know! Ambrosius said to stay here, to defend the mares."

"There's Fredek!"

The warrior unicorn squealed as a giant cat landed on his back. He bucked and kicked, snaking his head around to bite the cat, but its claws were in deep.

Crunch! The cat snapped the unicorn's neck.

"No!" Lily screamed.

"Poor darling Fredek," Chloe sobbed. "It's awful!"

Three fighting cats raced directly for the girls, giant fangs gleaming white.

"Round them up!" yelled Sasha. "Turn them back to us!"

"Come on!" Lily yelled at Chloe. "We can do it!"

Side by side, they galloped their ponies at the cats, swinging their sticks desperately as the cats' huge claws slashed out at the ponies' legs.

"Take that!" Lily's stick connected with the biggest cat as it swiped at Rainbow.

She swung the pony round on his haunches to block the cat's attempt to flee. "It's turning!"

Working together, swinging and striking with their sticks, she and Chloe edged the cats away from the young guard by the trees and into the path of a furious, sweaty Sigvard.

He didn't pause for a second, running his spike through the biggest cat. He chased down the next one and killed it with a furious stomp of his hooves.

The third cat ran, with Sasha in pursuit, until a roc plummeted from the sky, its massive claws raking at Sasha's head. Swiftly, she turned Tommy away, and the cat fled.

There seemed a brief lull in the fighting around them and they stood, watching and breathing hard.

"Lily!" Ambrosius galloped up, bloody wounds staining his silver legs and back. More blood – not his own – dripped from his horn. Lily gulped. This really was life or death.

"Guilio returns," said the unicorn. "It's time."

CHAPTER FIFTEEN

Lily looked up to see Guilio soaring towards her from the west just as Abellona resumed her attack with more fire bolts. Somehow the witch had another magic staff.

Bang! Whoomph!

Brökk responded to as many as he could, but Abellona had the advantage of moving more swiftly with Galen's powerful wings to carry her, compared to Brökk on the ground.

Lily gulped, terrified as she turned Rainbow away from the battle and her friends.

"You can do it, Lil!" Sasha yelled as Sigvard accompanied her and Chloe back to the young guard by the trees.

She hoped they would be okay.

She hoped she'd figure out how to complete this mission that Ambrosius seemed to think she could do.

How, she still didn't know.

But she was going to do her best.

The unicorns were counting on her.

She tried to get her bearings. There was the bush where the mares and foals were. The beach must be down there.

"Follow me!" Guilio shouted as he dodged another zilant attack. It was no safer in the air than on the ground. The pegasus sped away over a part of the forest she hadn't been in before.

She gathered her reins and sent her pony after the pegasus. "Run, Rainbow, run!"

As fast as they could, they dodged trees and jumped ferns and flaxes as the white pegasus flew slowly, skimming the treetops. Lily could keep him in sight most of the time, but it wasn't easy.

All of a sudden, Rainbow ducked around a fallen tree. Lily lost a stirrup and slipped sideways. Oh, help! She felt around with her foot for the dangling stirrup as the pony galloped on. Got it. She couldn't afford to fall off now!

They pushed on after Guilio, who slowed to hover in a clearing near a creek.

"Mikaela said she can scent Xanthe not far into those trees," he called. "Keep heading towards the beach. Good luck!"

And he left.

Rainbow plunged to a stop, and Lily looked around frantically.

They were all alone, and suddenly the forest was very quiet apart from the harsh sounds of their breathing.

Lily shivered. Being terrified reached a whole new level.

In the distance, she could just make out the thud of bodies, the screams of anger and clash of horns, the fierce battle not letting her forget for one second how important and urgent her mission was.

Slipping off Rainbow, Lily led him to the creek so they could both get a swift drink.

She swallowed the fresh water gratefully, but it didn't take away the bitter taste of fear that filled her mouth. The thought of going into those trees alone made her stomach knot even tighter.

Who or what would be guarding Xanthe?

How was she meant to actually reach Xanthe?

Crouched among the rocks and ferns beside the creek, something occurred to Lily.

The taniwha that Kuia mentioned. It's a full moon tonight, the taniwhas' favourite time to come out. They live in rocks near water, right? Didn't Kuia say something about them being guardians of the land, protecting it against enemies?

Would they help her?

Dare she ask?

And then the words simply came. In Māori. Calling on the taniwha to help protect their land from the magical invaders.

Quietly at first, she sang her karakia.

"Taniwha, oh Taniwha, Ka ahei au i te pātai ki a koe mō tō āwhina? (Taniwha, oh, taniwha, may I ask for your help?)"

Then she stood, and her message to the mythical creatures rang out through the forest. *"Kua tae mai tētahi mea kino kia whakamate ki tō tātou nei ao.* (Something evil seeks to destroy our land.)

"Ka taea e koe te āwhina ki ahau? (Can you help me please?)

"Āwhina mai kia tiaki te whenua. (Help me protect our land.)

"Āwhina mai. (Help me.)"

How Lily knew the right words, she had no idea – but in her heart, in her soul, she knew they were right.

But would the taniwha listen?

There was a rustle beside her.

The rock moved!

Oh my, it's changing shape!

A huge lizard-like creature stepped towards her, its forked tongue and beady eyes nearly level with her face, it was so big.

She edged back against Rainbow's shoulder. *It knows they aren't invaders, right?*

It watched them closely, each second like an eternity before it looked away at another rock making the transformation.

One after another appeared, until six taniwha surrounded Lily and Rainbow, their forked tongues flicking in and out as they scented the air.

Breath tight in her chest, Lily waited to see what they would do.

All six watched her with beady, yet not unfriendly eyes.

"Perhaps they're waiting for me to do something," she whispered to her pony.

Okay. She took a deep breath. *I asked them to come and they did. So now let's find Xanthe.*

"Come," she called to the great scaly lizards as she mounted Rainbow. She headed to the trees where Guilio said Mikaela got the strongest sense of the captive pegasus.

Rustling and slithering across the clearing, the taniwha followed Lily and her pony. Rainbow kept turning his head, eyeing the strange creatures suspiciously. But they followed without looking like they were going to attack, so Lily felt relatively sure she and Rainbow weren't in any danger from them. She only had Xanthe's guards and the possibility that Abellona might return to worry about. Only! She smiled grimly. She still had a lot to do.

The bush was dark, and it was impossible to progress

through it quietly, especially with six giant lizards fanned out behind them.

An eerie howl made Lily and Rainbow freeze. She looked around anxiously, as the taniwha kept moving, step by step in the direction of the howl.

"Must be Xanthe's guards," she whispered as she nudged Rainbow forward.

Then there was furious barking, and she urged Rainbow faster.

They burst into another clearing and she saw two huge fighting dogs and a wooden cage containing a pale shape. Was that the captive pegasus?

The taniwha were stationary, positioned around the edge of the clearing. They hadn't turned back into rocks, had they?

How could she get to the cage with those gigantic dogs in the way?

Rainbow sidled nervously as the dogs' barking got angrier.

Without warning, one dog flung itself at the pony.

"No! Get off him!" Lily yelled, as she wheeled Rainbow away from the attack. A taniwha rushed towards them but wasn't fast enough to stop the enormous dog biting the pony's hind leg.

With an angry squeal, Rainbow lashed out with both legs, dislodging his attacker. His next kick connected with the dog's head, leaving it motionless among the ferns of the forest floor.

The second dog attacked the taniwha, who simply snatched the dog's leg into its mouth. The dog tugged and howled. It bit savagely at the taniwha's face with no affect. The taniwha simply didn't let go, and the dog was trapped.

Lily looked down, trying to see Rainbow's leg. "I hope it's not too bad, Rainbow. We have to get to the cage!"

They crossed the clearing, jumping ferns and grasses as fast as Rainbow could go.

"Xanthe!" Lily called as she leapt down from her pony.

The pearly white pegasus lifted her head as much as she could and whickered.

The cage was so small, the poor, beautiful winged horse was forced to lie down, her head and wings squashed in on her body.

"Oh, poor Xanthe." Lily reached through the wooden rails to stroke Xanthe's face. "How can we get you out without hurting you?"

Quickly, she went around the cage. There didn't seem to be a door on any of the sides. "How did you get put in here?"

"Abellona built the cage around me using magic," the pegasus said sadly. "Only magic can open it."

Lily thought for a minute. "The taniwha are magical creatures and also very strong." She turned to the closest one. "Taniwha, can you help, tēnā? Please?"

Using its massive mouth and strong jaws, the taniwha grabbed a cage bar and twisted it away from Xanthe.

For a moment, it looked like the cage would resist the taniwha's powerful grip.

Then the wood splintered.

"Yes!" Lily urged. "Go on! Break them all."

The taniwha snapped one bar after another along the front of the cage.

"Thank you! Thank you!" Lily shoved the splintered timber out of the way. "Is it enough, Xanthe? I don't want the roof to fall on you."

"I think so," the pegasus replied. "I'll try."

Inch by inch, Xanthe crawled on her knees until finally she was free of the cage. Her wings were squashed with the feathers broken and every which way.

Lily cradled Xanthe's head as big tears welled from the pegasus's eyes.

"You're free."

"Thank you." Xanthe let her head rest in Lily's arms. "I can't believe it."

"Thank the taniwha."

"But you knew how to call them. To draw on their magic to go up against Abellona's strongest captive spell."

"Xanthe," Lily's voice quavered with relief now Xanthe was free. "I had no idea what I was doing. And I was terrified."

"No, you were brave, so very brave. We all thank you."

"The others!" Lily looked up. "How will we let them know that you're free?"

"I will call Galen." The pegasus trembled all over as she tried to stand.

Lily stood beside her but didn't know how to help. "When did you last eat or drink?"

Wobbly, but standing, Xanthe said, "Some time ago, but I'll drink when Galen knows." She groaned as she unfurled her cramped wings and flapped them tentatively before resettling them on her back. Feathers started to settle into place as she attempted to neigh. Xanthe coughed. "My voice is weak."

"If you can survive being Abellona's prisoner, you can do this." Lily rubbed the pegasus's neck in encouragement.

Xanthe neighed again, stronger.

Rainbow joined in, and together their voices rang out across the forest.

An answering call was faint in the distance.

"Galen knows I'm free!" Xanthe's face showed her joy of hearing her mate calling her.

Suddenly, there was an almighty shriek of rage.

"That must be Abellona!" Xanthe cried. "She can no longer control Galen!"

Lily looked up to see Galen and Guilio soaring side by side into their clearing. Laughing and crying from happiness, she ran towards the pair as they landed.

"Galen! You're here! Where's Abellona now?"

"Lily, you did it!" Galen's voice was just like Guilio's, but happier than she'd ever heard the herd's guardian pegasus. "Sigvard has her pinned down."

An almighty trumpeting neigh sounded through the forest, and Ambrosius's voice rang out. "The herd of Västerbotten has defeated Abellona!"

"Oh my god, oh my god!" Lily danced around Xanthe and Galen standing side by side, his wing over her bruised and broken body. Guilio's eyes were bright with happiness too as he trumpeted another victorious neigh back to Ambrosius.

Lily stopped. "Now what?"

She'd forgotten her pony. "Rainbow! Your leg!" She ran to him. "Let me look." She led him into a bright patch of moonlight.

The bleeding had stopped, and he wasn't limping, thank goodness. Hopefully there wasn't any serious damage. She'd treat it when they got home. First, they had to get back to the herd and see how she could help.

"I hope Sasha and Chloe are okay too," Lily said as, slowly, she, Rainbow and the three pegasuses – followed by the slivering taniwha – headed back to the others on the battlefield. They stopped for everyone to drink at the creek, and Lily expected the taniwha might go back to their rocks, but they kept following.

Cheerful whinnies grew louder as they navigated the trees.

Lily kept wiping tears away. She had been so scared! Could it be true that Abellona was now a captive of the herd she had pursued for so long?

Happiness for the unicorns was all mixed up with concern for what happened next. How would they keep Abellona safely captive so she couldn't hurt anyone else?

Poor Xanthe. Her knees and hocks were bleeding badly, but the pegasus said she would not stop until she saw for herself that Abellona was no longer a threat.

Lily racked her brain for which herbs could help Xanthe heal more quickly. Maybe Kuia could be encouraged to make a special tonic. She wondered what her mother would say about Rainbow's injury.

They reached the herd at last. Poor Xanthe was exhausted.

Lily ran to Sasha and Chloe, and hugged them tight. "You're okay!"

"You did it! You saved the unicorns!" Chloe was crying and laughing at the same time. "Are you hurt or anything?"

Sasha's grin couldn't be any wider. "It's amazing, Lil! You're amazing."

She nodded, unable to speak without bursting into tears again. She didn't know how she'd been able to call the taniwha. Perhaps she would never really understand. It had just happened. But she didn't say anything.

"Lily." Ambrosius's deep voice rumbled at her shoulder. "How will we ever thank you?"

She turned to fling her arms around the unicorn's neck. "I'm just glad you're alright."

"Most of us, yes." His beautiful face and strong legs were stained with blood and gore, and Lily could sense a great tiredness underlying his happiness. "Sadly, we have lost a few of our herd, and most of our warriors are injured in some way."

Abellona's furious shrieking interrupted them. Sigvard and Isak had her pinned to the ground, as she fought and struggled to free herself. The unicorns pawed the ground savagely with every shriek.

"Just give me a good reason why I can't run my spike through this evil creature," Sigvard growled.

Ambrosius sighed. "Because she's going to help us find Celestina."

Lily's eyes fixed on the witch who'd hunted the unicorns to the other side of the earth. Abellona's dark red hair was tangled, her dark robes muddied and torn. She didn't stop twisting and turning, trying to tug her robes away from her unicorn guards.

Lily trembled, as the horrible reality of the fears she faced in the last few hours struck her. What was wrong with Abellona that she sought to enslave the creatures she had once protected? Why had she become the way she had?

Lily thought of Abellona's twin brother Perseus and how the twins battled for so many years, yet briefly collaborated to capture their younger sister, all for the greed, the twisted desire to trap the unicorns.

She placed her hand on Ambrosius's shoulder, drawing strength from his closeness, from the fact he was okay. It was still amazing to think that they'd stopped the witch, that Abellona's magical powers had been so severely diminished when the spell over Xanthe and Galen was broken that the unicorns had been able to capture the witch, instead of the other way around.

"Thank goodness the unicorns are safe from you now," she whispered to herself. She wiped away the tears she didn't know had fallen and turned to the unicorn king. "Ambrosius, are you sure she can't do magic?"

"No, Lily, she's trying, but we have seized her last remaining enchanted staff and with her arms pinned down, she can't release any damaging spells the only way she knows how. However, she might make us all demented with that screeching." He turned to Brökk, who looked as weary and bloodied as everyone else. "Can you not come up with a silencing spell, please, Brökk?"

"I wish that I could, but I just don't have it in me, Ambrosius." The mage looked at Lily. "You have some powerful magic of your own, young one. Who are these creatures you bring with you?"

Lily turned to the taniwha standing in a group, watching them. "These are mighty taniwha, Brökk. Defenders of our land who came when I called."

"How did you do it, Lily?" Ambrosius whuffled warm breath over her hair.

"I don't know." The emotion she felt, so deeply, so real, when she called the taniwha rose up through her. She blinked as more tears threatened to fall. "The words, a karakia, just came out. Kuia would probably say our ancestors came to me and helped."

"Then we also owe them a debt of gratitude, Lily, for they helped us achieve something we could not do on our own," said Ambrosius. "Your instincts to travel to this faraway land were right, Brökk. There is, indeed, ancient magic here."

Wiping away the tears she could not stop at Ambrosius's words, Lily smiled. Everything had come out the way it was meant to. Just like Kuia always said.

She turned to the taniwha. "*Tena koutou.* Thank you. You have helped us defeat a great enemy, and we are forever grateful." She paused, thinking for a moment. "Could you do us one more favour, please? Hold the prisoner while we tend to the injured unicorns?"

The silent taniwha flicked their tongues, then walked towards the witch and the unicorns holding her captive. Abellona's shrieks reached a new level as the taniwha took hold of her legs and arms, and dragged her away into the trees.

"Not too far, please," Lily called. "We'll come and find you when we've got some way of holding her."

Light was just beginning to show on the horizon when Lily had used up the pots of salve and bottle of tonic. With Chloe and Sasha's help, they'd treated as many wounds as they could, and washed unicorn faces clean of the horror of fighting in the life-or-death battle. Brökk didn't have a lot of magical energy left, but enough to stop the bleeding of some serious wounds. Mikaela shared her special energies, standing with noses touching with those who were weakest.

"Isn't it awesome to see Xanthe with Galen?" Chloe said as they walked back to where the ponies were grazing near Ambrosius.

Xanthe couldn't yet fly, but Galen and Guilio kept taking to the air, swooping and diving over the herd in delight.

"Awesome doesn't begin to describe it." Lily grinned, then yawned so hard she thought her jaw might crack. "Wow, tired doesn't begin to describe how I'm feeling either. I could sleep for a month."

Yawning, Sasha said, "Me too."

"You must go home," said Ambrosius when they stopped beside him. "We will put Abellona into the cage in which she held Xanthe and block the end with branches. I have already had several volunteers to stand guard."

"Could she magic herself out?" Lily asked.

"Without Galen and her staff, her magical abilities are sorely impacted. Brökk is strong enough to maintain a captive spell over her for the moment. When we return to our homeland, we will consult with our brethren as to how she will be restrained long-term."

Lily nodded. She was too tired to think of anything except getting home safely before her family woke up. "Oh, there is one other thing. What will you do with the taniwha when you put Abellona in the cage?"

"We will express our most sincere appreciation for their assistance and let them return to their isolated creek in the forest."

"Say thank you from me too." Lily yawned again. "We'll try and come back to see you tonight."

"We would love that, but I believe we'll rest for a whole day at least. Perhaps you should too."

Lily hugged Ambrosius, and his warm breath ruffled her messy hair as she nodded. "Take your brave ponies and go home, girls. And thank you once again."

CHAPTER SIXTEEN

The ride back through the forest seemed to take forever. The ponies dragged their feet, and Lily struggled not to slump in the saddle. She was worried about the cut on Rainbow's hind leg.

"What am I going to tell Mum about Rainbow's leg?" she asked as they went through the gate into the home paddock. A sudden gust of wind swept her words away and the pines behind them creaked and groaned.

"I don't know, Lil, sorry," Chloe's voice was sleepy. "It wasn't as dark as it usually was among the trees, was it? We didn't even need a unicorn's glow."

Lily yawned. "Look how light the eastern horizon is. That's because the sun will be up soon. Well, it would be if it wasn't cloudy."

"Oy, Chloe!" Sasha pushed Tommy closer to Angel as Chloe wobbled sideways off her saddle and yanked her pony's reins. "You can't fall asleep yet."

Chloe rubbed her eyes. "Oh, sorry, Angel." She patted the mare's neck. "How am I going to get home once I leave you at Lily's?"

Lily tried to make her brain think, but it wouldn't co-operate as the wind swirled around them, lifting the ponies' manes. All she could manage was to sit silently on Rainbow's back, swaying with his long stride.

"Sleep at Lily's for an hour or so, then go home and say we've been out for an early morning ride." Sasha grinned. "It wouldn't be lying, because it is very early morning."

"I guess," replied Chloe. "I almost don't care what my mother says at this point."

"But you will if she threatens to sell Angel again."

Chloe jolted upright. "Oh, don't say that, Sash! That's awful."

"Just making sure you don't go and do something silly when we've managed to sneak out all these nights without our parents finding out."

The wind brought a cold, fine rain as they reached the barn. Lily slid, aching and sore, from the saddle and had to clutch onto Rainbow to stop her legs buckling under her. "Will you be okay riding home along the road, Sash?" She spoke quietly as she opened the gate from the yard onto the driveway for her friend, who always seemed to keep going no matter how tired she was.

"I'll be fine. See you sometime tomorrow. I mean later today." Sasha lifted a hand in farewell and disappeared into the grey and wet pre-dawn light.

"Come on, Chloe, let's get the ponies unsaddled and our gear away." Lily undid Rainbow's girth. "Can you help me with the barn door so it doesn't bang open in this wind?"

Chloe slipped off her pony. "The wind's horrible! I hope Sasha and Tommy are okay." She pulled the saddle off. "That wind's cold when the ponies are still hot. Have you got a spare cover I could put on Angel?"

They wrestled with the big barn door. "Rainbow's old one would probably fit, but if Mum or Dad come down to the horses before we wake up, they're going to wonder why the ponies have covers on when they didn't last night."

"Oh, yeah." Chloe put her tack away. "Not thinking." She yawned. "Too tired."

"You and me both. They'll go under the trees anyway with this rain. They'll be fine. We'll take a couple of slabs of hay for them to share with Gracie."

"Okay, good idea."

Lily trudged back to the barn as the rain fell harder, struggling to see if they'd left everything tidy.

Barn closed. Gate closed. Garden path. Back steps. Boots off. Tuck them at the back so no one could see they were wet.

Quietly, carefully, they tiptoed down the hall to Lily's room.

Thump!

Chloe stumbled against the wall.

They froze, hearts pounding.

"That you, Lily?" Mum's sleepy voice drifted down the hall.

"Sorry!" Lily hissed. "Just been to the toilet."

"Go back to bed then."

"Yes, Mum."

She closed her bedroom door. They were home at last. And the unicorns were safe. *Thank goodness.*

Chloe wrapped her in a hug, her mouth by Lily's ear. "Sorry."

"No worries," she replied.

Somehow, they managed to get Chloe's wet clothes

hanging up in the wardrobe without making any noise. Lily left hers in a pile. "Here's a t-shirt for sleeping in. And a pillow." She crawled into bed, Chloe at the other end, topped and tailed.

Lily stared out the window briefly. It was nearly dawn, but the heavy clouds and rain made everything darker than when they'd ridden home. *That wind isn't slowing down either*. It swirled and crashed around the house. *I hope the ponies and the unicorns will be okay*.

Thump! Thump!

"Illy!"

Lily kept her eyes shut. *Go away, Liam*.

She was so tired. So much had happened last night. *It's still raining*.

Her eyes snapped open and she sat up. *Chloe!*

Chloe was still here, asleep at the other end of the bed. *Shoot!*

"Go away, Liam!" she growled. "I'm trying to sleep." Lily shoved the covers off. "Chloe!" she whispered urgently. "Wake up!"

Chloe groaned. "Nooo... Go away." She rolled away from Lily.

"Come on, we've slept too long! You have to go before my family realises you're here."

Out the window, lightning flashed through black clouds as thunder boomed overhead.

"Oh!" Chloe's eyes opened, then she hid her face in the pillow. "Don't care."

Lily knew Chloe hated thunder, but somehow they had to get her home and fast. "You do care. What's your mum going to say?"

Chloe lifted her head to look out the window. Thunder rumbled and the rain came down even harder. "Darn."

"Chloe Cho!" Lily hissed. "I've never heard you curse before." She tugged Chloe's clothes off the hangers. "Now, get out of bed and get home before we all get into trouble!" Her friends couldn't be more different. *Sasha would have loved this weather and wanted us all to go out in it!*

Grumbling and mumbling, Chloe put her clothes on. "They're still wet."

"And they'll be even wetter before you get home."

"But Lil, how am I even going to get home in this weather? I'll drown if I don't die of fright from the thunder."

Lily plopped down on the bed and sighed. "You're right. It's a disaster. You should have gone home last night."

Chloe stood at the window, her face glum. "But I was so tired. I couldn't have walked that far."

"Darn." Lily repeated Chloe's curse word as she thought. "Oh, what if you climb out the window, sneak around the house and come in the back door as if you've been to see Angel?"

Chloe lifted her head, her lips curved in a hopeful smile. "And say what? Something like would I be able to get a lift home?"

Lily nodded. "Or phone your mum and say you're staying here until the rain stops."

"Worth a try, anyway." Chloe zipped up her jacket as thunder and lightning cracked simultaneously overhead. "God, I hate thunder!" She pushed the window open. "See you in a minute."

The wind carried rain in before Lily could get the window shut. Now she was drenched. "Darn," she repeated to herself. "I may as well get dressed now."

She pulled her bedroom door open just as her mother

said, "Chloe!" in a surprised voice. "What on earth are you doing here so early? And in this weather too."

Lily zoomed into the kitchen to see Chloe absolutely streaming water onto the doormat. "Oh, Chloe, fancy seeing you here!" she said while trying not to grin.

"I came to check on Angel with this awful weather, Mrs Masterton." Chloe shot Lily a pained look. "Could I call my mum to come and pick me up, please?"

"Of course." Mum turned to Lily. "Get a towel and some dry clothes for Chloe, Lily. She can't stand around so wet and cold."

Sprinting to the bathroom for a towel, Lily heard her mother say, "Were the horses under the big trees?"

"Yes." Chloe sniffed, then coughed as she hung her wet jacket on a hook.

"Come in and stand on this mat," Mum instructed. "I'm sure they were just fine, tucked in there."

"Seemed to be." Chloe coughed again as she rubbed her hair dry with the towel Lily passed her.

"Who's coughing?" Kuia's creaky voice drifted in from the hall as she shuffled slowly along.

"Chloe is, Kuia." Lily went to give her grandmother her arm to cross the lounge without her walking stick.

"Fetch a bottle labelled kumarahou tonic, Lily, my love." Kuia sat down heavily at the dining table. "This rain doesn't do my rheumatism any good."

"Haven't you got a tonic for that, Ma?" Lily's mum asked as she helped Chloe get her wet hoodie over her head.

"Of course, Tessa, but not with me." Kuia took the bottle Lily brought and shook it. "Measure out two table-spoons into half a glass of warm water. It doesn't taste very nice, Chloe, but it will help if you're getting a cold."

Now dry and dressed, Chloe took the glass from Lily and sipped. "Yuck! Do I have to drink it?"

Lily couldn't help laughing. She knew how awful some of Kuia's herbal things tasted.

"You better, or Kuia will just go on." Mum bustled around getting breakfast things out. "It might taste better if you eat something."

Chloe sat down at the table with Lily to start on cereal and milk.

"Mum, where's Dad and Liam?"

"Feeding out to the cattle."

"Oh, they're out early!" *Lucky we made it to bed before Dad got up!*

"Dad's off to that cattle sale up north right after breakfast."

"Okay." Lily crunched a mouthful. Gosh, she was tired. And worried about the unicorns and Rainb... "Chloe, your mum!" Her spoon clattered into the bowl.

"Oh, no." Chloe's face went pale. "I've been thinking of some other things."

"Me too." Running to grab the phone, Lily knew exactly what Chloe meant. What was happening with the unicorns? Were they okay after the battle and then the storm? How or when would she and her friends get to see the unicorns again? *I should have run down to see Rainbow as soon as I got up and checked his leg!* "Here, call."

Chloe went over to the sofa as she dialled. "Hello Māmā."

Lily could hear Mrs Cho's angry voice as Chloe held the phone away from her ear.

"I came to check on Angel, Māmā, and I did not want to wake you. Sorry, I forgot to leave you a note."

Chloe rolled her eyes as she looked at Lily. Her mother kept talking and talking.

"I'm okay, Māmā. Lily has lent me some dry clothes."

Her mother continued.

"I will come home when the rain stops." And then she sneezed.

Lily's mother lifted her eyebrows as the volume of Chloe's mother's concerns grew louder.

"Thanks for being a chilled-out mum," Lily whispered.

Her mum kissed Lily on the head as she got up to put more toast on.

Chloe put the phone back on its stand. "She's coming to pick me up in ten minutes. She says I cannot always be eating my meals at your house. It is not right." She sneezed again. "I do think I'm getting a cold. My head's sore too."

"How about a painkiller with your breakfast?" Mum reached into the pantry. "I'm sure your mother will think that's okay."

"Yes, please." Chloe sank into her seat. "I'm so tired."

"Sounds like you need a quiet day resting in bed." Lily's mum handed Chloe a pill and a glass of water.

"Thanks, Mrs Masterton. I've got a piano lesson today, so I'll have to practice first."

"Hmmm," was Mum's response as she turned to talk with Kuia.

"I'll check on the ponies after breakfast." Lily hugged Chloe gently. "They'll be fine." She crossed her fingers and hoped. "I'll message you later."

"Thanks, Lil." Chloe sneezed, then sighed. "I'm not much use, am I?"

"You can't help being sick, and I won't be doing much outside today anyway." Lily lowered her voice, hoping Mum wasn't listening. "It's too dangerous to ride through the forest when it's this windy, for a start." She was longing to see the unicorns, but how? She only hoped they'd manage it before the unicorns decided Brökk was strong enough to create the chasm back to their homeland. She didn't want to think how awful it would be to never see Ambrosius again.

A knock on the door interrupted her thoughts.

Mum opened it. "Come in, Mrs Cho."

"No, no, I just come for my daughter." Chloe's mother said in her clipped English. She wore a big rain jacket, but she still looked very wet. With a snort that was sort of a laugh, Mrs Cho added, "Some time I think she rather live here than in her own home."

Lily stared down at her empty bowl. She didn't dare look at Chloe. She knew Chloe would often rather be at Lily's place because Chloe had said so. They'd all ride a lot more together if Mrs Cho allowed it. But she didn't.

"Hello, Māmā." Chloe got up, pushed in her chair, and took her plate to the dishwasher. "I'm sorry to disturb your morning."

"So you should be. Going off in weather like this. Crazy, I told your father."

"Bàba is home?" Chloe smiled. Her father was away a lot with work.

"Yes, for now. Let us go." Mrs Cho held out Chloe's wet jacket. "Say thank you."

"Thank you, Mrs Masterton," Chloe said politely, as she let her mother put the jacket on. "I'll talk with you soon, Lil. Thanks for checking on Angel. Goodbye Kuia."

"Talk soon." Lily smiled at her friend. "Goodbye, Mrs Cho."

"Yes, bye." Mrs Cho ushered her daughter out just as

Chloe sneezed. "Oh, now you are sick, are you?" She shut the door firmly.

Lily could hear Mrs Cho's voice over the wind and rain until the back gate banged shut. Poor Chloe. Her mother wasn't easy.

"Mum, I'm just going to run down and check on the ponies, then could I have toast and a hot chocolate in front of the TV for a bit? I didn't sleep well with this storm."

"Why not?" Mum agreed as she made more tea for her and Kuia. "Not much else to do on a horrible day like this. Put all your wet weather gear on, won't you?"

"Of course. And thanks!"

CHAPTER SEVENTEEN

Tears rolled down Lily's face, merging with the pouring rain. "My poor Rainbow."

What she thought was a cut on his leg was actually a deep gash.

And her beloved Kaimanawa pony was lame.

Very lame.

Rainbow stood, his head dropping so he could rub his muzzle on her shoulder as she crouched to look at his injury. The depth and width of the wound was starkly obvious against his bay coat. White flesh showed inside the gash, washed clean of all blood by the constant rain.

"No Pony Club Championship qualifier for us." Lily sniffed as she stood. "But there's not much point crying, is there?" She sighed as she patted the pony's sodden neck. "We did what we needed to do to help Ambrosius, and now we just need to get you well. Come on, can you walk up to the barn? Mum needs to see your leg, then I guess this week's pocket money will be a contribution to getting the vet here."

Lily sighed again as she tugged Rainbow gently by the

forelock to get him moving across the paddock to the barn. He limped with each slow step.

"Oh, buddy, I'm sorry it hurts so much. How did you get us home this morning? I'm sure you weren't limping. Mum and the vet will help make you better. I just hope it being washed clean by the rain was a good thing, not something that might mean it gets infected."

Step by step, they trudged wetly across the paddock, the other ponies following right at Rainbow's tail, not wanting to be left behind.

"Horses get injured in storms all the time, right?" she said to Rainbow. "It's not like Mum's going to think it's unusual or something else might have happened. I hope so, anyway."

She opened the gate just enough to let Rainbow through and shut Gracie and Angel out. Gracie objected with a loud whinny as her friend limped to the barn. "I'll come back with some hay for you two and Kahurangi once I've got Rainbow sorted."

Leaving Rainbow in a stall with hay to nibble on, she sploshed back to the house to get her mother.

Lily had a long wait for her toast and hot chocolate, but eventually the vet had been to put a few stitches in Rainbow's leg, bandage it up, and administer painkillers and antibiotics. Kuia gave her a tonic to help cuts and bruises, and Lily had made up the first dose for Rainbow to drink. Then she'd splashed across the horse paddock and back with hay for all the horses before checking in on Rainbow in the barn.

"You okay, buddy?"

He seemed happier, munching his hay like normal.

"Hopefully the drugs are helping." She checked his water and pulled stray bits of hay out of it. "But I can't ride you for a month!" She pushed her wet fringe out of her eyes. "Well, the main thing is you get better properly and maybe Mum will let me ride Gracie some days with the girls. That's if you don't mind, of course."

She rubbed around his ears the way he liked.

He nodded then turned around carefully before lying down in the stall's deep layer of wood shavings. "Guess you're ready for rest. I'll see you later, okay?"

With a last pat, she closed the stall door before leaning on it.

A whole month of no riding and no training! We really will have to start all over again with our show jumping. Oh, well, at least Mum didn't ask how Rainbow got hurt. I wasn't lying when I said I didn't see it, because I really didn't!

The buzz-buzz of a text message woke Lily. Her hot chocolate had gone cold, and the TV was muted. She rubbed her eyes and yawned. It was Chloe, asking how Rainbow was.

"Ok." Lily wrote back. *"Wound deep. Stitched up now. He's resting. Can't ride him for a month!"*

"Glad he's ok, but a month!?? Oh no!" Chloe replied.

"Sucks, eh?"

"Yeah, but amazing none of the rest of us were hurt last night."

"True. How r u?"

"So tired."

"Me too."

"Piano lesson soon. Better go."

"C ya." Lily yawned as she put her phone down. She

snuggled back into the sofa cushions and let her eyes close. *I wonder how the unicorns are with this weather. I know lots will be injured but I can't do anything to help this time. It's so frustrating. I hope Brökk will have plenty of magic to heal everyone, and I guess Mikaela helps too.*

Thump, thump. Someone knocked on the back door then let themselves in.

"Hello, Sasha." Lily's mum's voice reached Lily from the kitchen. "Kind of wet to be out, isn't it?"

"Yeah, but I'd rather be wet than at home, so...here I am."

Sasha reached the sofa and Lily sat up. "Gee, a drowned rat has nothing on you."

Sasha pushed her sodden hair back from her face. "Who cares? Tell me what's been happening."

Lily pushed herself up. "Come on. We'll go to my room and I'll grab you a towel on the way."

They sat, cross-legged, facing each other on Lily's bed.

"You all right?" Sasha rubbed her blond hair with the towel.

"Rainbow's leg is really bad." Lily sighed. "Can't ride him for a month."

"A month! What about the qualifying competition?"

"Can't do it, can I?"

"Oh, man... That sucks." Sasha threw the towel at the closed door.

"Tell me about it."

"He'll be okay, though, right?"

"The vet thinks so. It's a deep cut, but more of a flesh wound than anything, so it should heal up fine. Might be a scar. Kuia gave me a tonic."

"Poor Rainbow." Sasha sighed. "This rain!"

Lily looked out the window. It was just as gloomy and grey as it had been all morning. "I know. Are you okay?"

"Tired."

"Same."

"It's awful at home, Lil. Like I told your mum, I'd rather be walking in the rain than stay in the house one second longer."

"Arguing?"

"Yeah. Non-stop." Sasha's eyes filled with tears.

"I'm really sorry, Sash." Lily leaned over to hug her friend. "Can I do anything to help?"

"Let me stay here until I'm like 18."

"Um...we'd have to ask Mum and Dad."

"I'm joking, Lil!" She tried to smile. "Wish I wasn't, but let's talk about what's really important. How are we going to get back to the unicorns to check they're okay?"

Lily looked out the window again. "Even if the rain doesn't stop, I think we have to try and go tonight, don't you?"

"But how, Lil? You don't have a pony."

"I'll ride Gracie."

"Really?" Sasha lowered her voice. "But what if something happens to her? What would your mum say? How many times have you ridden her anyway?"

"What's the alternative? I run beside you and Chloe?"

"I guess not." Sasha went over to the window. "Seriously, how many times have you ridden her?"

"Once."

"Lily!" Sasha hissed. "You can't ride a strange horse – your mother's horse – through the forest, where we're not meant to go without permission anyway, at night and in weather like this."

"Seriously," Lily echoed her friend, "what other option do I have?"

"Oh boy... I don't really know." Sasha perched on the edge of the bed. "Do you think Chloe will come? She's so scared when she has to sneak out of the house."

"Shall I ask Mum if you can both stay here tonight?"

"Great idea, if Mrs Cho will let Chloe."

"I'll text her. Then do you want to come check on Rainbow with me?"

"Of course."

The wet afternoon dragged on. The only person happy about the rain was Lily's father, because all the farm paddocks were getting a good watering.

In a hushed voice, sitting cross-legged on the floor of her room, Lily told Sasha how frightened she had been when she'd freed Xanthe.

"I don't know how you did it, Lil."

"You and me both." Lily looked out at the greyness. "How did I know what words to say? How did the taniwha hear me? How come they've never emerged from their rocks for any other reason?"

"Because you just did. And didn't Ambrosius or Mikaela say something about there being ancient magic here? Abellona was threatening the people of this land – you – so they came to help."

"Yeah, they did say something like that. I don't know if they meant Whale Bay or the whole country though."

"Probably both." Sasha shifted to lie back on a pillow and stare at the horse posters Lily had pinned to her bedroom ceiling. "You're the one with Māori blood. There are lots of Māori myths and legends, right?"

"Just because I'm part Māori, doesn't mean I understand them, Sash."

"You should ask Kuia."

"Hmm. I could, but what do I say? Kuia, have you ever seen a taniwha? Because somehow I managed to summon six from the rocks of the big creek." She laughed, then became serious again. "Maybe it's just one of those things we'll never really understand."

Sasha sighed. "Like how I'll never understand how two parents who loved each other enough to get married and have two children now fight every second they're together."

Lily squeezed Sasha's hand. "Kinda different, but just as confusing."

Sasha pushed herself up. "I guess I better go home and get Tommy, my toothbrush and stuff."

Lily jumped up. "I'll come with you, and we can check on Rainbow on the way."

"I'm going to ride Tommy back."

"Yeah, so I'll bring my bike and ride with you."

The rain stopped suddenly as they walked down to the barn to see Rainbow. He was still lying down, but his leg didn't feel hot or swollen which would have been a sign of infection. They gave him clean water and fresh hay, and left him to rest in the barn overnight.

At Sasha's, no one was home.

"Blissfully quiet," said Sasha as they went up to her room.

"Did your mother text you to say she'd be out? Or leave a note?" Lily asked.

"Doubt it." Sasha screwed her face up in disgust. "My

mother doesn't bother about things like that. Not like yours."

"But..." Lily stopped herself saying anything that might upset Sasha further. "Never mind. Want me to go get Tommy in while you pack your things?"

"Good idea." Sasha grabbed her backpack off the floor. "Let's go before anyone gets home and starts fighting again. I'll text Dad to say I'm at yours. Then at least one of my parents knows where I am, right?"

"Sure." Lily felt fake as she smiled, then headed back downstairs. She thought Sasha often made things worse with her mother, but she didn't know what to say. And she felt guilty for having such a nice, normal mother, one who never used emotional blackmail – which is how Sasha described some of the things her mum did.

Sasha's parents had a big, fancy house on a small block of land, only just big enough for Tommy. They bought a lot of hay for Tommy from Lily's dad, and the bright chestnut gelding was tugging hay from his hay net under a wooden shelter when Lily reached him.

"Hey, Tommy." She smoothed a hand down his neck. "Ready for another midnight ride?" she whispered.

The pony nickered as she slipped his halter on.

"A quick brush and I'll saddle up."

Sasha decided to lead Tommy, so they walked along the muddy roadside path back to Lily's.

Sasha looked up at the fast-moving clouds. "I wonder if we'll get more rain. How do you think the unicorns are doing?"

"It's hard to know, isn't it? That's why we have to go tonight whether it's raining or not."

Lily's phone beeped. "It's Chloe. She can't come

tonight. They're going to a concert in the city, and she doesn't know when they'll be back."

"Oh, darn." Sasha sploshed through a muddy patch beside Tommy.

Lily stopped to read the message properly. "She says I should ride Angel."

"That's a good idea. At least Angel knows what she's doing on these night rides. And you're not risking your mother's horse."

"But..." Lily jogged to catch up. "Angel is worth, like, thousands of dollars."

"So?" Sasha turned Tommy into Lily's driveway. "If she offered Angel, you should ride her. Chloe only wants to try and help."

Lily thought for a moment. "True." She sighed. "I thought capturing Abellona would solve everything, but there's still so much we don't know. Will Brökk even have enough magic to get them home?"

"I don't know, Lil."

They watched TV for a while after dinner but were both yawning so much Lily's mother told them to go to bed.

"No argument from me," Sasha replied. "I'm whacked."

The quiet beep of Lily's phone alarm woke them at midnight. They dressed and left as silently as thieves, remembering to pick up the big torch. Lily closed the back door ever so slowly. *How weird that sneaking out at night is starting to feel normal.*

It felt even more weird to be catching and saddling Chloe's pretty palomino rather than her beloved Rainbow, but he was safely tucked away in the barn so wouldn't see her ride off on another pony.

Lily took a few minutes to settle into the rhythm of Angel's stride as they crossed the horse paddock. "Oh, her trot is long compared to Rainbow's, but she's so smooth."

"She is, eh?" Sasha latched the gate into the forest and Lily turned the torch to the track through the trees. "Chloe let me ride her a while back. She's really lovely."

The big paddock on the deserted farm looked much the same as any other night they'd been to visit. Baubles of golden light dotted around, each one showcasing a silvery unicorn.

"Wow!" Sasha pulled Tommy to a halt at the gate. "They are so beautiful, so magical."

"Yeah. We're so lucky to be the ones to see it." Lily looked for Ambrosius and Brökk.

"Lily! Sasha!" Ambrosius's voice rang out. He galloped towards them, Sigvard and Mikaela spinning to thunder after him.

"Where's Chloe? Is she alright?" Mikaela asked as the three unicorns pulled up in a flurry of wild manes. The unicorn glow burnished their polished horns with golden light.

"She's fine." Lily replied as she reached out to pat Ambrosius. "She's really sorry, but she couldn't come tonight."

"That's a relief," Mikaela replied. "We have enough injuries here without worrying about one of you three."

"Well, Rainbow can't be ridden for a month, but otherwise we're all okay," Sasha said.

"But he'll be okay?" Ambrosius asked.

"He will, thanks," Lily replied. "The injuries are the main reason we're here," said Lily. "We've bought more tonic and salves. Are you all okay? Is Abellona is safely locked away?"

"She is, Lily, thanks to you," said Ambrosius.

"Hear, hear!" cheered Sigvard. "Lily saved us from near certain capture this time."

"Well done, Lily!" called several of Sigvard's young guard now standing behind him.

"Thank you, Lily!" shouted another.

She blushed and looked down, embarrassed by the attention.

Ambrosius rubbed his cheek on her shoulder. "You really did save us, Lily. We are so very grateful for your courage and that you worked out how to free Xanthe."

Tears welled as Lily looked up at the unicorn king. "I still don't know how I did it."

"Dear heart," Ambrosius's voice rumbled with affection. "That doesn't make it any less worthy or any less successful."

Lily scrubbed the tears away. "I guess." She smiled. "The main thing is you're safe."

"And we are. Safer than we've been for many years. Thanks to you and your friends, and your brave ponies."

Lily's smile turned into a grin.

"You did good, Lil!" Sasha leaned over and patted her shoulder. "We all did! Come on, we've got bruises and wounds to see to."

They worked by the light of the unicorns themselves, as one unicorn after another came up to show them injuries from the great battle. With gentle fingers, Lily spread Kuia's healing salve around the edges of open gashes while Sasha measured out dose after dose of the tonic Kuia made to help cuts and bruises. Brökk created more healing spells, and Mikaela shared her curative energies.

It didn't take long before they ran out of Kuia's herbal remedies. "What a shame, but of course she thought she was making enough for just one pony, not a whole herd of unicorns," Sasha said.

Lily sighed. She really wanted to help a young unicorn with his shoulder slashed open from the giant fighting cats, but Ambrosius assured her that Brökk would help Tymek and the young warrior would be well soon enough.

"What would you normally have done to tend injuries, Ambrosius?"

"Until Celestina was captured, she would help Brökk heal those with serious injuries with magic."

"You must miss her."

"We do. Very much." He nodded. "And now Abellona is under our control, maybe we'll be able to find Celestina and free her. That's if we can outsmart Perseus. We have much work to do when we return to our homeland."

"Are you going soon?"

"We will leave before dawn."

Lily stared at the unicorn king, stunned and silent.

CHAPTER EIGHTEEN

"Tomorrow?" Sasha gasped. "Like the dawn at the end of tonight?"

"Yes, Sasha. The coming dawn," Ambrosius replied in a sombre tone.

She flung herself at Sigvard. "But I won't see you again!"

Lily's heart was heavy as she hugged Ambrosius. She knew the unicorns had to go, but it was so soon! "But how, Ambrosius? Are Brökk's magical powers strong enough to make the journey safely?" Imagine if they got stuck in the chasm and couldn't reach the other end!

"I will let Brökk tell you," rumbled the unicorn king, "for something unexpected happened when you freed Xanthe."

Lily and Sasha turned to the herd's darkest and oldest unicorn. He looked different somehow. Bigger. And more powerful.

"Well, as Ambrosius said, something unexpected happened." Brökk looked at the girls. "Abellona is a strong and forceful witch in her own right, and we knew that she drew extra power from Galen and Xanthe, for Galen told Guilio. We didn't know she drew power from the rest of her captive armies as well. The zilants, rocs and fighting cats she bought here. Dragons, other unicorns and pegasuses at home. She had some way of enhancing their enslavement spell so their enforced allegiance to her also created trickles of magical power. Many trickles of water make a great river at some point, you understand?"

"Wow," Sasha breathed. "So the bigger her army got, the stronger she became."

Brökk nodded. "Although we unicorn mages also grow in power as we age, she was growing much more powerful than my colleagues and I working together. From what we were told by the zilants, who are remarkably intelligent creatures by the way, freeing Xanthe also broke the enslavement charm. The leader of their flight, Zax, says they were also freed and can now choose to share their magical powers with whomever they wish.

Lily looked at Brökk in wonder. "And they choose you!"

The mage nodded. "They do. Until we are home or until such time as we may need to forge an allegiance again."

"That's amazing." Lily grinned. "Fantastic! You all get to go home! I wasn't sure that was ever going to be possible."

"Neither were we, Lily," Ambrosius replied.

Then something occurred to her. "Chloe won't see you!"

Ambrosius looked around for Mikaela nearby. "Mikaela, it is your connection with a human. Do we stay another day so you can see Chloe again?"

Lily was stunned into silence again. Would the unicorns consider doing that?

As usual, Sasha's brain worked quickly. "We'll ride

home right now and go around to Chloe's to get her. Then you can leave at dawn as you planned."

"Can't you use your phone devices?" Sigvard asked of his favourite human.

"Chloe's mother doesn't let her have her phone in her bedroom," Sasha explained. "We'll have to try and wake her up some other way. It's not that I want you to leave, of course." She hugged Sigvard. "But I know you want to get home and see if you can find Celestina."

Lily's mind clicked back into gear. "Okay, we'll throw pebbles at Chloe's window or something to wake her up. But we still have only two ponies."

Ambrosius spoke. "Where does Chloe live?"

"Along the main beach, around the headland from the small beach where you made the chasm."

"We will take your forest track as we can't pull Abellona's wheeled cage through the forest. I presume we can cross your farm to go down to the beach."

"You can, but you'd be seen from the house if anyone was looking."

"How likely is that before dawn?"

"Possible but not likely." Lily looked at Sasha who looked worried. "Mum or Dad could be up if Liam wakes, and Kuia often wanders around if she can't sleep."

Sigvard asked, "Is it far, from the forest gate where we have been meeting you, to the beach?"

"Not very far," Lily replied. "Around the lower slopes of the horse paddock and down the beach track."

"Do you think that a herd's worth of hooves would be audible by your people?"

Sasha said, "If the wind's blowing in from the beach like normal, it wouldn't. And obviously none of you would show your glow."

"So," Ambrosius jumped in, "the reason I asked where Chloe lives is, none of you really need to ride a pony to meet us at the forest gate, do you?"

"No," said Lily. "We can easily walk."

"Good!" His voice was brisk. "Off you go and get Chloe. We'll meet you at the forest gate in two hours' time. That will give us time to decide who will pull Abellona's cage first." He turned to look out over the unicorn herd gathered around them. "I suggest you all graze hard on this fine pasture and ensure you drink before we depart."

Mares and their foals started trotting off to fresh parts of the paddock. Lily could hear their teeth ripping the grass as they chewed as fast as they could.

"Go!" He instructed the girls. "Isak, accompany them to the gate!"

The tall sentry unicorn trotted up as Lily swung up onto Angel. "How are you feeling about them leaving?" she asked quietly as Sasha settled into Tommy's saddle.

"Sad, but happy if that makes sense."

"Yeah. Same." Lily sighed as she turned to watch the silvery unicorns under the moonlight. Isak touched noses with Angel, then spun away towards the driveway.

"Come on." Sasha pushed Tommy into a canter. "We don't know how long it's going to take us to wake Chloe up. You know how deeply she sleeps. Even Liam crying in the middle of the night doesn't wake her at your place."

Lily let Angel follow Tommy. "True!"

They made it back in record time, the ponies' hooves thundering through the pine trees behind Isak.

At the gate, he said, "I leave you now."

"Thanks." Sasha leaned to pat the tall Isak, but he spun out of reach and galloped back into the trees.

Lily slipped off Angel to deal with the latch. "I've never

thought about the sound of hooves being carried out of the forest to the house. I wonder if the wind has always been blowing so it didn't carry."

"Who knows?" Sasha nudged Tommy through. "Come on, I've got to get all the way home and walk back before we can go to Chloe's."

"I'll bike beside you, then you bike to Chloe's too."

"Good idea."

Angel got a thankful pat as they slipped her saddle and bridle off at the yard gate. The pony wandered off to find Gracie almost before they led Tommy into the yard by the barn.

"I'll keep going," Sasha hissed. "See you soon."

Lily put Angel's tack away, being as careful as she could with the creaky barn door. Then she crunched quietly across the gravel yard to her bike leaning by the garden gate.

As she pedalled after Sasha, she couldn't decide whether she was more worried about the possibility of the unicorns being seen or heard as they headed for the beach, or the risk of waking Chloe's mother or father.

"Crikey, if one of Chloe's parents catch us, all our parents will know we're out in the middle of the night anyway," she muttered to herself. "There'll be hell to pay whichever way you look at it." She pedalled into Sasha's drive. "We'll just have to make sure they don't hear us."

"Shssh!" Sasha hissed as Lily's brakes squeaked to a halt next to the shed Sasha's dad had built for Tommy's gear and hay.

"Okay, okay!" Lily hissed back as she waited for Sasha to shut the gate to Tommy's little paddock. "Where's your bike?"

"Up at the house."

"Come on then."

They walked silently on the tar-sealed drive.

Sasha whispered, "Lucky I remember to turn off the automatic sensor lights when I come out at night, eh?" She picked up her bike where she'd left it lying on the lawn.

"Good thinking."

Seconds later they were pedalling out of the driveway, heading back past Lily's and on to the main beach road where Chloe lived in a fancy house looking out to the ocean. It felt so weird, biking past dark and silent houses.

Lily's heart thudded as they stopped outside the imposing gates. She lay her bike down on the grass, Sasha copying her actions before holding a finger up to her lips. "I know," Lily mouthed.

Sasha fumbled with the latch on the small person-sized gate set into the big iron gates. With a clank loud enough to make Lily jump, she finally got it open.

"Thank goodness it wasn't locked," Sasha muttered as they stepped through.

They stuck close to the shadows as Sasha led the way around the house and looked up at Chloe's bedroom window.

"Her parents' room is around the front, right?" Lily whispered.

"Yup." Sasha looked around for a pebble on the immaculately swept path.

"There's some in this planter." Lily grabbed some and passed them to Sasha. "You try. I'm worried I'll smash something if I throw too hard."

"And I won't?" Sasha flung two little stones up to the second-floor window. Ping, ping! They bounced off the glass. "Chloe!" she hissed. Ping, ping went two more pebbles.

The curtains moved inside, then Chloe's head appeared as she opened the window.

"I'm amazed she woke up," Lily murmured.

"What are you doing?" Chloe whispered loudly.

Sasha replied, "You have to come. The unicorns are leaving."

Chloe didn't hesitate, even though Lily knew she'd be worried about sneaking out of the house again. "I'll meet you outside the gate." Then her dark hair swung inside, and the window closed silently.

Sasha tugged Lily's arm, and they walked carefully back through the shadows to the gate and onto the path.

It felt like ages as they watched Chloe's dark and silent house for any sign that she'd made it safely outside. A dozen scenarios played through Lily's mind, and she half expected Mrs Cho to come charging out of the gate, demanding to know what was going on.

Chloe suddenly appeared as an inky shadow, making Lily jump.

"What do you mean the unicorns are going?" Chloe whispered as she closed the gate without a sound. "How?"

"Let's walk." Sasha grabbed her bike. Once they were away from Chloe's house, she spoke quietly, filling Chloe in.

"That's amazing about Brökk's magic." Chloe's grin shone in the streetlights as they walked quickly along the beach road back to Lily's. "But I'm sad they're going so soon."

"I know," Lily sighed. "But the main thing is they are safe and are able to return home."

"True, but..." Chloe echoed Lily's sigh. "I wish I'd had the chance to get to know Mikaela better. To understand this connection we feel."

"I'm the same about Ambrosius," Lily said. "Isn't it crazy to feel happy and sad at the same time?"

"I know!" Chloe smiled. "They're so beautiful. I'll never forget them."

"Me neither."

"Me three," Sasha laughed. "You know what's really crazy – that we each formed a connection with a unicorn. That there were three unicorns in that one herd who would be extra special to each one of us."

"Sure is!" Lily grinned. "I'm so glad I decided I had to tell you both about the unicorns. I could never have kept them a secret from you, but you wouldn't have believed me if you hadn't seen them yourself."

Sasha shoved Lily's arm in a friendly way. "You mean we would never have forgiven you for not telling us! Come on, let's jog. We didn't think to tell Chloe to bring her bike."

"I could double Chloe."

"No, thanks!" Chloe was quick to respond. "My own feet are fine."

The girls jogged along the long stretch of Beach Road before turning into the rural road which led to Lily's and eventually Sasha's and the back route to town.

"Keep to the grass edges if you can," Lily said as they turned into her drive. "And we'll climb over the fence into the horse paddock, rather than going over the gravel in the yards."

Excited and nervous, Lily led the way over the fence and across the silver-lit pasture.

"It's quite weird being out at night without the ponies," she said quietly once they were partway across the paddock.

"Isn't it?" Chloe replied. "Was Angel good for you earlier?"

"Perfect." Lily smiled. "Thank you for letting me ride her."

"No worries. Thanks for coming to get me when you knew the unicorns were going."

"Of course!" Sasha exclaimed in a hushed voice. "How could we not?"

They reached the forest gate and waited, leaning on the gate to look into the darkness of the pines.

Little sounds of the still moonlit night seemed loud now that they'd stopped walking through the long pasture. Away through the trees, a morepork called, then something rustled in the grass nearby.

"What was that?" Chloe grabbed Lily's arm.

"A mouse or something, probably."

A harsh cry sounded in the trees.

"Gee, Chloe, don't squeeze my arm off." She eased Chloe's hand away and held it. "It's just a possum."

"Are you sure? It's not Abellona."

"I'm sure, right, Sash?"

Sasha nodded. "We didn't get too close, but Abellona is safely locked in the cage she used to keep Xanthe in. Brökk said the zilants helped him with some kind of spell so she can't move or speak. Or do magic, obviously."

Chloe sighed with relief. "Okay."

"Listen," Lily peered into the pines. The tread of many hooves sounded loud in the stillness of very early morning.

"Let's open the gate." Sasha dealt with the latch. Together they pushed the gate wide open, flattening the long grass growing up around it.

Ambrosius, Sigvard and Mikaela appeared on the stony forest track, leading the gilded herd towards the girls.

CHAPTER NINETEEN

L ily smiled as Ambrosius and his herd came closer, her
heart filled with happiness to see so many of them
looking well and strong. Brökk and Mikaela must have been
busy with their magical healing over the past couple of
hours.

Their three special unicorns stopped at the edge of the
trees, Ambrosius calling a halt to those behind.

"Come!" he called softly to the girls, who ran up the
track to meet them.

Lily stroked the unicorn king's cheek as he lowered his
head to her. Sasha had Sigvard's neck wrapped in a tight
hug, and she could hear Chloe murmuring to Mikaela.

He spoke in his rumbling voice. "We have stopped here
to be out of sight of the house. Thank you for opening the
gate. We want to be ready to move quickly and quietly
through it and across the paddock to your beach track. Now,
come over to this bank so you can climb on my back to ride
down to the sea."

"Really?" Lily looked at him.

He nodded and edged himself alongside the bank as she scrambled up. "Jump on. The others are waiting to do the same. It's a small treat in an effort to show you how much we appreciate your help."

"Wow, thank *you*!" Lily leaned out to take hold of Ambrosius's mane, then jumped. She was astride the huge unicorn once more! She stretched her legs down and inched forward to sit in the natural curve of his back. She felt like she and Ambrosius could conquer all the bad witches in the world.

Ambrosius stepped aside for Sigvard as Sasha got up on the bank, who grinned as she leapt onto the dark dappled grey warrior.

"You're letting me ride you after saying you wouldn't!" she exclaimed.

"True," Sigvard concurred, "but only because I agreed with Ambrosius that it was appropriate in such special circumstances."

Sasha laughed. "You've been wanting to do this as much as I have!"

Chloe slipped gently onto Mikaela's back. Her face lit up as she settled, taking a careful hold of the mare's long silvery mane.

Lily looked at her friends. All the worry of sneaking out at night, the intense fear of the battle with Abellona. None of it mattered now to see their smiles, to feel so happy herself. Like this was predestined in some way, what she was on this earth to do.

"Now." Ambrosius's voice brought her back to the present reality that the unicorns were leaving. "Sigvard and Sasha, please ride at the front to lead the herd in the most direct route to the gate down to the beach. Mikaela and

Chloe, if you can ride near the middle of the herd to keep an eye on young Tymek, Lily and I will close the gate and make sure those pulling Abellona's cage for this stage of the journey are comfortable. Remember, everyone trotting as quietly as you can. Make your feet light on this blessed land which helped us free ourselves from tyranny. On your command, Sigvard."

Ambrosius moved past the warriors, mares and foals, murmuring words of encouragement to several as they prepared to follow Sigvard in treble file.

They reached the four strong soldier unicorns harnessed to the wheeled cage containing the silent, spellbound witch. It was hard to believe that the small figure lying so still within the wooden bars was the same creature who had terrified them with her vicious lightning bolts just a couple of nights ago.

"All right?" Ambrosius asked of his soldiers.

"Yes, Sire," replied one at the front, lowering his voice to speak directly to the king. "She's given us no trouble, now that Brökk and Zax got that captive spell right."

"Excellent." Ambrosius glanced around at his human rider. "Are you okay, Lily?"

"Yes, Ambrosius. I'm not even very frightened of Abellona now."

He looked at the witch as Sigvard gave a silent signal for everyone to move forward and the unicorns pulled the cage away from them. He then started to trot a short distance behind the cage with Lily holding onto his curly silver mane to stop bumping around too much with his prancing stride.

It didn't take long for everyone to turn into the paddock. Lily slipped off Ambrosius's back to pull the gate shut, then climbed the gate rails to jump back on again.

"Lily," Ambrosius said solemnly as they followed Abellona's cage, "it is most important that you never underestimate her or her brother Perseus. At this moment, she may be mute and unable to move, but that doesn't mean she's not watching and listening."

A chill trickled around Lily's neck, making her shiver. *Oh, yuck, she might be watching me like she did before!* She wrenched her eyes away from the wicked sorceress and looked for Chloe and Mikaela riding further up the column of unicorns.

"There are two things I regret," Ambrosius continued in a hushed tone. "One, that we asked so much of you personally in the end. It required you to be dishonest with your parents and resulted in Rainbow being injured, and now you cannot compete in the competition that means so much to you. And two, that our combined actions to disable Abellona mark us forever as her enemy. Although we are used to this *status*, if you could call it that, I do not yet know what the implications for you might be. And this worries me."

Lily pondered Ambrosius's words as she watched the unicorns in front of them. Long rows snaked across the dimly lit paddock. Sasha and Sigvard were nearly at the gate which led through the bush down to the beach.

She moved with his stride, trying to soak up the feeling of riding the unicorn one last time. "Ambrosius, I will never regret anything about helping you. As Sasha often says, you and the herd are the most amazing thing to have ever happened to us."

"That is very kind of you to say, Lily, thank you."

"Rainbow will be okay soon, and there are other competitions. And if our parents never know about us going out at night, that will be okay too. But..." She paused to think.

"But Abellona?" he prompted.

"Can she hear us?"

The unicorn dropped back a few metres. "Definitely not now."

"What you said has me worried. Could she ever come back to New Zealand without Brökk's chasm?"

"I do not know, Lily, but that is why we will work on our allegiance with the zilants to keep Abellona safely locked away when we get home. Brökk has also suggested we try and find one of his brethren, a very old mage who has gone away to live a solitary life. She had a long history with Abellona and her twin brother, and their mother before them."

Lily jumped in. "So she might know other magic that can stop them?"

"We hope so, yes, if we can find Hakana."

Sasha and Sigvard were already through the gate and out of sight down the track. The unicorns followed as instructed.

"We haven't been paying much attention!" Lily said as she saw Chloe and Mikaela turn through the gate.

"The herd has done as instructed," Ambrosius said as he trotted to catch up with the unicorns pulling the cage. "You'll slow for this turn, yes?"

"Yes, Sire."

"You might need to walk down the track," Lily suggested. "It's quite bumpy."

"Yes, we will," the team's leader replied.

Lily slipped off Ambrosius to shut the gate. It took a moment for her eyes to adjust to the darkness among the trees on either side of the beach track, but then she could make out the silver unicorn forms moving as quietly as they could.

"If you stand here, Ambrosius, I can mount from that

post." She clambered up some rails beside the gate and slipped onto the unicorn's back for the last time.

He walked after his herd, and she leaned forward to lie over his withers, hugging his neck. Happiness and sadness rolled through her, and she closed her eyes, savouring Ambrosius's warmth and smell as her face pressed into the crest of his neck.

Nearly the whole herd was returning safely to their homeland – which was a good thing, but also sad. Sad for the unicorns who had died in the battle with Abellona and now lay buried under a mighty kauri tree near the battle-field. Sad for her and her friends who had grown to love the unicorns so very much in such a short time.

She sniffed away the threatening tears. It wasn't a time for crying. She should be happy that the unicorns *could* go home, right?

Lily sat up on Ambrosius's back as he walked down the steepest part of the gravel track. Ahead, she saw the unicorns moving around the sandy curve to the far end of the beach where Brökk's chasm had emerged.

"Will it take you three days to go back through the chasm, Ambrosius?"

"Brökk says not this time with the help of the zilants."

"Oh, I've been wondering how they get home."

"They should be here any minute."

And with that, she heard the swooshing rhythm of large wings approaching from the direction of the abandoned farm. The flight of zilants swung over the herd to land on the beach near Sigvard. Their wings settled with a slith-ering sound that made her shudder. *Imagine being right beside them like Sasha is.*

Then came the rocs, who now carried the giant fighting cats upon their backs.

"Are they all in allegiance with you now, Ambrosius?"

"Let's call it a work in progress."

Lily's gaze was captured by the magnificent sight of three pegasuses sweeping into land.

Lily grinned. "Oh, look, Xanthe is flying!"

"Indeed she is, my dear Lily, and all thanks to you."

Her heart filled with happiness, she leaned forward to hug the unicorn. "You're very welcome, Ambrosius."

"I feel as happy as you, dear child. Truly, we have a new era of life to return to and I do not know how we will ever repay you."

"Don't say that. You know I would do anything to help you all. Seeing Xanthe flying with Galen and Guilio might just be the most amazing thing I've ever seen." She paused, thinking of the night she first saw the unicorn king. "Except that moment when you galloped up to me and Rainbow on this beach. That..." She blinked away sudden tears. "You...you are absolutely the most beautiful creature I have ever seen."

"Ah, Lily." Ambrosius nuzzled her knee. "I will miss you very much."

Tears plopped onto Lily's jeans before she wrapped her arms around his neck once more. "Oh, I know! I will miss you heaps!"

Shrill whinnies interrupted their conversation.

"Ambrosius, the cage!" Lily pointed to the wheeled cage, which was bogged in soft sand despite the muscular efforts of the four harnessed unicorns.

A harsh cry was followed by four zilants leaping into the air and racing to the cage. Quickly, they formed up over the cage, grabbed the roof bars with their massive talons and flapped their wings. The combined efforts of the flying serpents and the unicorns soon had the wheeled crate back on firm sand.

"That was impressive!" Lily said as Ambrosius carried her close to the zilant leader.

"Our squads are well drilled," replied Zax in his heavily accented tones. "Just part of our new collaboration with the herd of Västerbotten."

"Much appreciated," Ambrosius bowed his head. "Brökk. Zax." He looked to the magic-makers. "It is time to go. The portal please."

The darkest grey unicorn – looking more powerful than she'd ever seen him – stood with the steely-grey serpent. Together they intoned a deep chant in a language she did not understand. With a roar, the chasm into the sand opened.

This was it. Lily had to say goodbye to Ambrosius, to all the unicorns and the pegasuses.

She blinked hard, her eyes brimming. Where were Sasha and Chloe?

"Sasha is near, and I will call Mikaela to bring Chloe," Ambrosius said.

Astonished, Lily managed to say, "How did you know what I was thinking?"

"Our connection is stronger than you realise. If you think of me when I have returned home, you will know I am thinking of you."

"For real?" Her mouth quivered.

"For real," Ambrosius chuckled as he repeated her words.

Mikaela trotted briskly towards them, and Ambrosius turned to join Sigvard and Sasha in front of the chasm.

"Girls," he said solemnly. "It is time."

Lily slipped off the unicorn king's back and hugged his

head as he lowered it to her. "Goodbye, Ambrosius, I will never forget you."

"Nor me, you, darling Lily. Remember what I said about us thinking of each other."

"I will." She wiped tears from her cheeks. "Travel safely."

"We will," he replied. "Brökk and Zax will look after us well."

Lily stepped back, away from the unicorn, as Chloe stumbled away from Mikaela. "Come here, Chlo." Lily wrapped her friend in a hug, then felt Sasha's arms go around both of them.

"We knew they had to go," Sasha mumbled into Lily's shoulder. "But that doesn't make it any easier."

"I know," Lily sniffed as she lifted her head. "Look, Sigvard is leading them into the portal."

Sigvard had a group of warriors around him. He reared high. "Farewell, Sasha," he called before spinning to plunge into the dark swirl of the chasm opening, his warriors with him.

Mares and foals. The guard of brave young unicorns. The four pulling Abellona's wagon.

"Goodbye, Chloe, farewell." Mikaela disappeared with her injured Tymek.

In groups of three or four, the unicorns headed into the portal to the other side of the world.

"Haere ra, Lily!" Ambrosius spoke in the language of Lily's forebears.

"Goodbye, Ambrosius, goodbye," she whispered as the unicorn king went out of sight with the three shining white pegasuses. Zilants and rocs flew low and fast into the chasm's swirling dust. Only Brökk and the zilant leader were left on the beach.

"Thank you! Farewell!" Brökk called.

Then they were gone.

Whoomph.

The portal vanished, and only messed-up sand near the high tide line remained.

"Oh," Chloe sighed sadly. "They're really gone."

"Gone, gone, gone." Sasha started walking back along the beach. "Time to go home and back to real life, I guess."

Lily grabbed Chloe's hand as they ran after Sasha. "But we three will always know the unicorns are real." She took Sasha's hand as well. "We will always know how special our connection was. That we saved them from a life as Abellona's prisoners."

"Yeah." Sasha sounded upset. "You're really the one who saved them."

"I couldn't have done it without either of you!"

"Okay, but we'll never see them again, will we?" Sasha grumbled.

"Who knows?" Chloe asked as they climbed the bush track. "Who knew any of this would happen, yet it did!"

"I guess," Sasha agreed with a sudden flash of grinning teeth in the gloom. "And now we've got a long walk home seeing as Lily and I are walking you back to your place to make sure you get in safely."

"We are?" Lily asked.

"We are. Because there is absolutely no point us having gone out all these nights if we can't all make it home undetected after one last adventure." Sasha let Lily's hand go and twirled up the bush track. "Wasn't it amazing? Riding the unicorns!"

And that was what they talked about all the way home.

"Can you believe two weeks ago we were saying goodbye to the unicorns?" Chloe whispered in Lily's ear as they watched Sasha and Tommy clear another show jump.

"No, not really," Lily whispered back. "Weird how it starts to feel so long ago, like a fairy-tale or something, eh?"

"So weird. Like being able to sleep through the night without worrying about whether I'd wake up in time to come and meet you guys."

Lily's eyes moved with Tommy as he cleared the final jump. "She's done it! She's qualified!"

"Woohoo!" shouted Chloe.

They clapped and cheered with Lily's mum as Sasha galloped Tommy around the ring, grinning fit to bust, before turning her chestnut gelding through the entrance back to her friends.

"You did it, Sash!" Lily beamed as Sasha flung herself off Tommy to hug her friends before turning back to her pony.

Sasha let Tommy's girth out and rubbed his sweaty brow. "Only because you couldn't compete on Rainbow."

"No way!" Lily shook her head. "What do you think, Mum? Sasha rode brilliantly, didn't she?"

"You did very well, Sasha." Lily's mum ran her hands down Tommy's legs. "This pony is a credit to your hard work and talent."

"See, you deserve to go to the championships!" Lily laughed. "I'll take you on next year, don't you worry!"

Sasha looked at Chloe. "I'm sorry you didn't get through, Chlo."

Chloe smiled. "It's fine. It was my fault, not Angel's. When I told Mum, she said I could have more lessons if that's okay with you, Mrs Masterton."

"Of course, Chloe, I'm happy to help," Lily's mum replied.

The loudspeaker interrupted.

"Come on, Sash," Lily straightened Tommy's wayward mane. "You better mount up and go get your red ribbon!"

THE END

GLOSSARY

Glossary of New Zealand and Māori words

Bush – native forest or areas of native trees, shrubs and plants

Kaimanawa pony or horse – come from a population of feral horses which live in the Kaimanawa Ranges in New Zealand. They are descended from domestic horses released in the 19th and 20th centuries. They are known for their hardiness and quiet temperament.

Kuia– Māori for grandmother, female elder

Mokopuna – Māori for child

Kawakawa – a small native tree with bitter leaves

Rongoā – traditional Māori medicine, a system of healing passed on orally

Over-faced – when a horse is asked to do something it doesn't have the experience or training to do

Roc – an enormous legendary bird of prey in the popular mythology of the Middle East.

Zilant – a legendary creature with the head of a dragon, the body of a bird, the legs of a chicken, the neck and tail of a snake, the ears of a canine, red wings, sharp teeth, dark-gray feathers and scaly dark-gray skin.

Karakia – Māori incantations and prayers, used to invoke spiritual guidance and protection.

FREE GOODIES TO SAY THANK YOU

Hello, and thank you for reading *Lily and the Unicorn King*.

I hope you enjoyed this book as much as I enjoyed writing it.

A free factsheet on Ambrosius

It's been fantastic fun, creating the unicorn characters and dreaming up their world. If you'd like to know more about Ambrosius, the unicorn king, and the quests ahead of him in future books, simply visit BookHip.com/HQHCAX to download the factsheet. It's a PDF file so should be readable/viewable on all devices and computers.

Free downloadable posters!

Would you like free posters of Ambrosius, the unicorn king; his lieutenant, Sigvard; and the sensory unicorn, Mikaela?

Then I invite you to join my readers' list, if you haven't all ready, and I'll email you the links to the three digital posters created by my wonderful illustrator and fellow New Zealander Emma Weakley which you can download to print, save on your device or computer or simply enjoy.

Head over to www.kategordonauthor.com and follow the readers' list link on the homepage.

I also share reviews of other great pony stories and other books I've enjoyed – you might enjoy them too! There will be giveaways from time to time, and other fun things celebrating our shared enjoyment of reading a good book.

Reviews

Can I ask you to review *Lily and the Unicorn King* please?

I truly value your feedback on this story. You're welcome to email me – books@kategordonauthor.com or if you would like to post your review via the online bookstore where you purchased the book or on your favourite book review website, that would be ideal.

I appreciate your time and effort, thank you. All reviews – negative or positive – are an important aspect of building the profile of every book. You probably look at reviews before you buy a book, so you can help other readers decide if *Lily and the Unicorn King* is a book that they or the younger readers in their life might enjoy.

ABOUT KATE

Kate Gordon spent 90% of her childhood reading books about ponies. The other 10% she spent galloping around the garden on an imaginary horse – until she was able to ride a real pony of her own.

Now she's penning fantastical adventure stories about brave friends, ponies and unicorns.

Kate is inspired by the magical mountains of Central Otago in New Zealand's South Island where she lives with her husband, three dogs, and two cats. She's currently working on her second book in the Unicorn King series and would love to tell you when it's ready – join Kate's readers' list to be the first to know!

Photo by Vicky Fulton

Connect with Kate online

facebook.com/KateGordonAuthor

instagram.com/kate_gordon_author

To my husband Jeff, who always believed I could finish this book. Thanks, darling, for keeping on asking if I should be writing.

ACKNOWLEDGMENTS

Writing this story has been harder and taken longer than I could ever have imagined.

It's also been a lot of fun, spending time lost in my imaginary world of unicorns, ponies and brave young riders.

Another fun aspect are the wonderful people I've met on this writing journey.

To my original writers' group Shar, Wendy, Cheryl and Trudie, you guys fuelled my passion to write fiction, so thank you! I just needed to find my own path with children's fiction. I'm rapt to see you all being so successful as indie authors.

To my Society of Children's Book Writers and Illustrators critique group, thank you for all your helpful feedback and constructive criticism. I loved reading your amazing stories.

To my Central Otago writing friends Maria and Rose, I always love talking writing with you. It's such a treat!

Thanks so much for sharing the ups and downs of this journey.

To my writing wizard buddies, Elena, Amanda and Jess, you're all amazing! Wonderful women and writers. I'm loving the opportunity to focus on middle grade fiction, to support and encourage each other, and bounce ideas around. So many cool things to learn and discuss!

To my illustrator Emma Weakley, you have done an incredible job translating my ideas into stunning visuals. Thank you, most sincerely.

And to Rose from A to Z Book Cover Design, you've taken Emma's illustrations and created book covers that I am incredibly proud to show to the world. Thank you!

A special thanks to Flynn Rosie for helping with the Māori translation.

To all my friends and family who asked, 'how's the book going?', thank you. Please keep asking that question as I start work on the next book!

COMING NEXT

SASHA AND THE WARRIOR UNICORN

A family crisis. A call for help. Can she support her dad while joining the unicorns' rescue mission?

Sasha's parents are heading for the divorce court and her dad needs her. Then the warrior unicorn appears, trampling her mother's prized garden, and asking her to help him rescue their imprisoned protector...in Scandinavia!

But the unicorns' time travel spell doesn't work. She misses an important meeting for her dad. Sigvard is relying on her to complete his quest, but so is her dad. She doesn't want to let either of them down.

Can Sasha risk time travelling to help Sigvard fight his way to their snow-bound protector and get back in time for the court hearing?

Sasha and the Warrior Unicorn is the second book in the Unicorn King middle grade fantasy series. If you enjoyed *Lily and the Unicorn King*, you'll love the second instalment when Sasha, Lily and Chloe risk all to help their beloved unicorns.

Make sure you know when *Sasha and the Warrior Unicorn* is released. Sign up to Kate's special readers' list via www.kategordonauthor.com.

Thank you!